"Why don't we grab a cup of coffee and discuss what, exactly, you want me to do?"

Eric's proposition caught Jenny off guard. *Oh, if only you knew,* she thought. Jenny brought her attention back to the situation at hand.

This was a bad idea. But it wasn't about her. This was about a bachelor auction for charity and she had to think less like an adolescent with her first crush and more like a mature adult.

A woman who turned to mush while looking into the warm, chocolate-brown eyes she could easily get lost in.

Exercising tremendous self-control, Jenny forced herself to remember what she had to do later that day. "Sounds good to me," she said, slowly peeling the words off the roof of her mouth one by one.

Jenny looked away from Eric's smiling face. She had to. There was no other way she could possibly regain the use of her legs.

MARIE FERRARELLA

earned a master's degree in Shakespearean comedy and, perhaps as a result, her writing is distinguished by humor and natural dialogue. This RITA® Award-winning author's goal is to entertain and to make people laugh and feel good. She has written 155 books, some under the name Marie Nicole. Her romances are loved by fans worldwide and have been translated into Spanish, Italian, German, Russian, Polish, Japanese and Korean. Marie loves working on a continuity because it makes her feel part of a great, satisfying whole and there's nothing like teamwork to make you feel vital and alive.

LOGAN'S LEGACY

THE BACHELOR

MARIE FERRARELLA

Silhouette® Books

Published by Silhouette Books
America's Publisher of Contemporary Romance

Special thanks and acknowledgment are given to Marie Ferrarella for her contribution to the LOGAN'S LEGACY series.

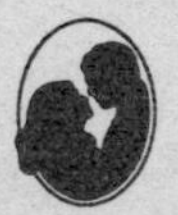

SILHOUETTE BOOKS

ISBN 0-373-61388-1

THE BACHELOR

This edition published by arrangement with Harlequin Books S.A.

Visit Silhouette Books at www.eHarlequin.com

Printed in U.S.A.

Be a part of

LOGAN'S LEGACY

Because birthright has its privileges and family ties run deep.

She had a crush on a billionaire playboy who had no intention of settling down...or so she thought.

Jenny Hall: She couldn't remember a time when she didn't love Eric Logan. But when her colleagues bought her a dream date with him, she found herself tongue-tied—and wondering how their worlds would connect.

Eric Logan: On a break from his life of fast jets and corporate boardrooms, Eric strutted his stuff at a bachelor auction...and became sweet Jenny Hall's date for one night. As he entered *her* world, he realized his bachelor days were numbered!

Who's the mysterious woman at the bachelor auction? Peter Logan can't take his eyes off her...and has no idea that this beauty will soon make a serious impression on his heart!

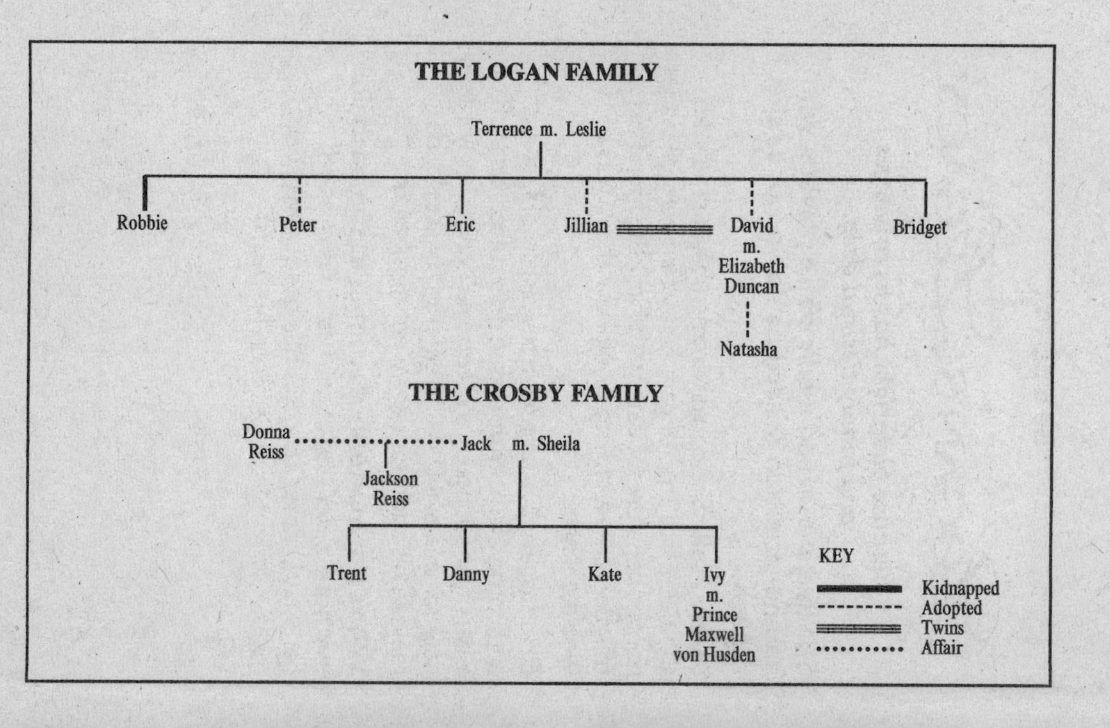
THE LOGAN FAMILY
Terrence m. Leslie
Robbie
Peter
Eric
Jillian
David
m.
Elizabeth
Duncan
Bridget
Natasha
THE CROSBY FAMILY
Donna
Reiss
Jack
m. Sheila
Jackson
Reiss
Trent
Danny
Kate
Ivy
m.
Prince
Maxwell
von Husden
KEY
Kidnapped
Adopted
Twins
Affair

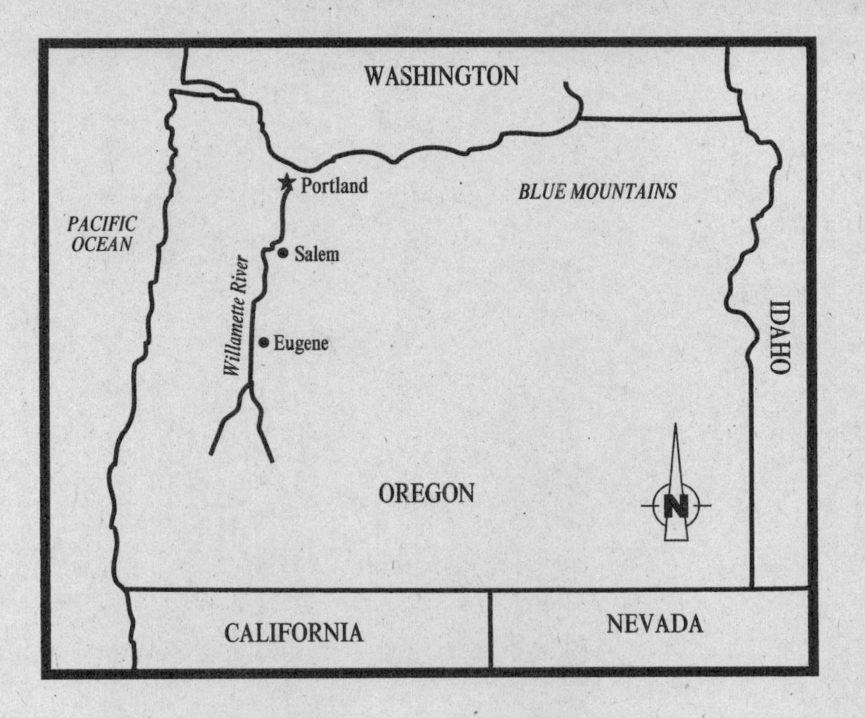
WASHINGTON
Portland
BLUE MOUNTAINS
PACIFIC
OCEAN
Salem
Willamette River
Eugene
IDAHO
OREGON
N
CALIFORNIA
NEVADA

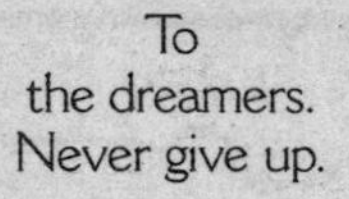

To
the dreamers.
Never give up.

One

Elaine Winthrop Hall hooked her Donna Karan-clad arm through her daughter's, and accompanied her into the living room. Jenny knew her mother was trying hard to keep from commenting on Jenny's shapeless sweatshirt and her small apartment.

Jenny called the room cozy; her mom called it tiny, pointing out that she had bigger walk-in closets. But square-footage meant nothing to Jenny.

Neither, her mother was always quick to interject, did prestige, breeding and other people's opinions. People who counted.

Elaine's perfectly made-up eyes slanted a glance at the small four-year-old boy who sat on the carpet in the middle of the room, silently playing with an imaginary friend. Jenny knew Cole was the reason she'd come to these crammed quarters, to once more try to talk some sense into her "obstinate" daughter's head.

The woman didn't have to speak for Jenny to know what was on her mind. It was all fine and good to let your heart rule once in a while, she'd say, but that should involve the matter of men over the height of three feet, not small "anchors" that would only get in the way of the family's best-laid plans for the future of their only daughter.

Elaine finally spoke, modulating her voice to something that could pass as a stage whisper. "He's not your problem, Jennifer," she insisted not for the first time. "He's not your responsibility."

It had been a very long, very stressful day, following on the heels of other equally long, equally stressful days. Jenny surprised herself by finding an untapped vein of patience. She always tried to keep an ample supply under the heading of "Mother," but she'd been pretty certain that she'd exhausted the allotment on their last visit.

Nice to know some of the patience had managed to regenerate itself.

"He is not a problem," Jenny told her mother softly but firmly. "And he *is* my responsibility. I gave my word to a dying woman."

This was not news to her mother. Jenny had already said as much several times over when she'd explained to both of her parents why she was adopting the once sunny child. Jenny studied her mother's perfectly made-up face, searching for a hint that the milk of human kindness was not a myth, but existed within the breast of the woman she, despite so many shortcomings, really did love.

She tried again. For the umpteenth time. "What would you have me do, Mother, go back on that? Go back on my word? You were the one who taught me to honor my commitments, remember?"

The woman sighed. "To honor them, yes, but you keep this up and you'll be the one being committed. To an institution." She glanced again at the little boy and shook her head. "There are places for children like Cole. Lots of people would love to adopt him. He's still viable."

"Viable?" Jenny stared at her mother in disbelief. "He's not a plant, Mother, he's a little boy. A little boy who's been through a great deal, who saw his mother die." What did it take for her mother to finally get it? She was Cole's last chance. If she couldn't get through that protective wall he'd constructed around himself, no one could. "You want me to run out on him, too?"

Elaine pressed her lips together. Jenny knew her mother didn't like coming off as a villainness, but the woman had been shaped by decades of adhering to rules and regulations about what was permissible and proper, all of which prevented her from even leaning toward her daughter's side.

Casting the boy a glance, the older woman said, "I'm not saying run out on him exactly, just give him to a family. A traditional family." Jenny knew that her mother had never approved of one-parent families. In Elaine Hall's world, you began with a husband and wife, then you introduced children into the setting. Anything else was unpardonable. Her mother had nearly had apoplexy when she'd told her about adopting Cole.

"You know, Jenny," the woman continued, "You're not SuperWoman."

Jenny hated having limits applied to her, hated all the rules her mother lived by. They were like something from another century. "Just because you don't want me to be doesn't mean it's not so."

Elaine paused, looked at her oddly, then shook her head. "You always could confuse me with your rhetoric."

Jenny grinned. "Call it a self-defense mechanism." Her stomach rumbled, reminding her that she'd skipped lunch and the dinner hour had already arrived and was in jeopardy of leaving. "If you wanted to browbeat me, Mother, you could have e-mailed."

Her mother frowned, transforming her attractive face into a weary one. "What I want is for my daughter to find her rightful place in the world."

Translation, Jenny thought, what her *mother* deemed to be a rightful place. They were worlds apart when it came to that. Her mother didn't approve of Jenny's career, her apartment, her almost monastic lifestyle. Not that the latter had much appeal for her, either, but until they found a way to create more hours in the day, dating and men were just going to have to stay on the back burner.

Jenny tried to keep her voice cheerful. "News flash, I have."

"What?" Elaine fisted her hands at her waist and forgot all about her stage whisper. Cole looked her way and she dropped her voice an octave. "In that awful legal aid firm, housed in a building with faulty electrical wiring and bad plumbing?"

Trust her mother to hone in on the bad points. But the firm had to be where the poor people were, not in some upscale building in the best part of Portland. "We took the landlord to court over that," she informed her mother, then added proudly, "and won."

"What is wrong with being a lawyer in a respectable, well-known firm? What's wrong with trying to make money?"

Jenny straightened the newspaper she'd left in disarray that morning. Other than that, nothing was out of place in the apartment. Cole was in preschool most of the day. When Sandra, her baby-sitter brought him home, Cole rarely touched any of the toys Jenny had bought for him. They remained in the toy box, leaving her nothing to tidy up now. She was forced to look at her mother as she fought the good fight and tried to remind herself that she wasn't ten years old anymore.

"Nothing is wrong with making money," she replied. "I'm trying to make it for my clients."

Elaine's frown deepened. "I meant for yourself."

"I don't need much money." Leaving Cole in the living room, she moved into the kitchen, several steps away, and began getting out dishes in anticipation of calling out for a pizza. Her mother had arrived just as she was about to dial the phone, postponing the order. "Haven't you heard, Mother? The best things in life are free."

Elaine scoffed. "It wasn't true when Al Jolson sang it, and it's not true now." A note of desperation entered the woman's voice. "This is breaking my heart, Jennifer. You're wasting your talent and your life."

Jenny felt sorry for her mother. They were never going to see eye to eye about this. "My life, Mother, my talent."

Elaine closed her eyes, momentarily retreating. "Your brother told me this was a waste of time."

At the mention of Jordan, Jenny grinned again. She needed to get in touch with him and soon. "My brother, at times, is wise beyond his years." She thought of a way to usher her mother out without resorting to anything physical. "Want to stay for dinner? I was just about to order a pizza."

Elaine cringed. A pizza had yet to ever cross her perfectly shaped lips. "I have an engagement."

This time it was Jenny who hooked her arm through her mother's and very gently escorted her toward the door. "Of course you do. Don't let me keep you from it." Separating herself from her mother, she opened the door. "Your mission was a failure, Mother, but it was nice seeing you."

Crossing the threshold, Elaine paused long enough to turn around and shake her head. "Do you realize that there are girls who would kill to have your background and opportunities?"

And if she didn't, Jenny thought, there was her mother to remind her. Endlessly. To her credit, she didn't roll her eyes. "By all means, Mother, give it to one of them before someone gets hurt."

Elaine drew herself up. "Everything isn't a joke, Jennifer."

"No," she admitted, although heaven knew both her parents could do with a little more humor in their lives, "but if you smile, you can get through anything." She leaned forward and brushed a dutiful kiss against her mother's cheek. "Smile once in a while, Mother. It keeps the lines at bay." And then, straightening, Jenny took pity on her mother. "If it makes you feel any better, I'm chairing the annual bachelor auction again for the Parents Adoption Network. Some of your society ladies are bound to be there, drooling over the eligible studs who'll be parading around."

Elaine's eyes narrowed. "Don't be vulgar, Jennifer. A lady doesn't drool."

Jenny held up an index finger, begging to differ. "A lady doesn't let anyone *see* her drool," she corrected with a grin.

In the face of undeniable defeat, Elaine squared her shoulders, a determined soldier to the end. "You are impossible."

Jenny cocked her head. "Yes, but I love you and

you've got another one at home to work your magic on."

"Jordan doesn't live at home, Jennifer. He hasn't for years now. You know that."

Her mother had always been a stickler for precision. "Figure of speech, Mother," she said as she began to close the door.

Elaine stopped her for one last-minute order. "Eat something."

Jenny held up her right hand, taking a solemn oath. "The moment they deliver it," she promised, then closed the door quickly just in case her mother changed her mind and found something else to criticize. She leaned against it, looking out toward the living room and Cole. "That woman spreads joy whenever she goes." She sighed, straightening, then walked into the living room. "She doesn't mean anything by it, Cole. She's really got a good heart.. It's just hard to find under all those layers of designer clothes and jewels."

She glanced through the window. It faced the parking area and she could see her mother getting into her car, assisted by the chauffeur. Jenny tried to remember if she'd ever seen her mother actually driving a car, but couldn't.

"It's true what they say, you know, the rich are different from you and me." She nodded as if the boy had responded. It was something she did each evening in the hopes that someday she could coax more than a word or two at a time out of him. A precocious little boy, he'd talked all day long—until his mother had died. "Right, I know what you're thinking. That I'm one of them, but I'm not. You can't hold the accident of birth against me, you know. I didn't ask to be part of the elite and I got out as soon as I could."

Which was true. She never felt as if she fit into her parents' world, not really. The girls her mother wanted her to socialize with were so shallow, so vapid. She had more of an affinity for the people she was trying to help, but she didn't quite fit in their world, either. Jenny sighed quietly. There were times that she felt like a fish with feet. She could swim in one world and walk in the other, but fit in neither.

"The privileged think just that—that it's a privilege for anyone else to look upon them. They don't realize that floating from cocktail party to cocktail party around the world doesn't lead you to discover the true meaning of life."

Cole merely went on playing with his imaginary friend as if she hadn't said anything at all, but she tried to convince herself that the sound of her voice was comforting to him somehow. She remembered the boy he had been until six months ago, a bright, sunny child who laughed all the time. But he had been very attached to Rachel and her death had hit him very hard.

Almost right after the funeral, when the death had finally sunk in, he withdrew from the world. He hardly spoke at all, but he screamed in his nightmares, calling for Rachel, pitifully sobbing out "Mommy" over and over again.

She would rush into his room and hold him until he'd fallen back asleep again, her own heart breaking. Someday, Jenny promised herself, someday, she was going to reach him. Until then, she would go on being there for Cole.

Jenny glanced at the kitchen table where the file she'd brought home lay spread out, covering every square inch of surface. She was in the middle of a court battle on behalf of Miguel Ortiz. If she won, it would go a long way to easing the man's life. It would never, barring a miracle, put him back on his feet again, or free him from the endless pain he'd been subjected to ever since a highly respected and highly inebriated surgeon had worked less than magic on his spine, but it would pay for Miguel's bills and allow the man to regain some measure of self-respect.

They were getting closer to the end now. For the last five weeks, she'd done nothing but eat, sleep and breathe the case, but she needed to steal a little time for herself. And she could think of nothing better than creating a tiny island of time where she could share herself with the one person who truly mattered to her. Cole.

Bending over, she gathered the towhead into her arms and drew him close as she stood up again. Jenny kissed the top of the boy's head.

"Don't you worry about what the Wicked Witch

of the West said. I'll always be here to take care of you. You and me against the world, kid, right?" He raised his head to look at her with Rachel's soft green eyes, his expression never changing. "Of course right," she murmured softly. "C'mon, we'll order that pizza and then I'll read you a story. I think we both need to unwind after that surprise visit."

In her heart, she knew her mother meant well. For that matter, both of her parents did. But there was no way she was going to give up any part of her life. She loved being a champion for people who had all but lost hope. And she loved Cole. More than anything, she wanted to be a mother to him.

If there was a part of her life that didn't feel quite right, that felt as if there was something missing, like a supportive prince to turn to in times when her spirits flagged and she desperately needed bolstering, well, whose life was perfect anyway? Hers was close to it as far as she was concerned, and that was enough.

Juggling the child and the phone, she placed her call to the local pizza parlor. On a first-name basis with most of the people who worked there, she asked Angelo for an extra large pizza with extra cheese and three kinds of meat. He promised to deliver it within the half hour.

"There," she told Cole, hanging up, "that should hold us."

Going to the small bookcase in the corner, she selected a book she knew was a favorite of Cole's and sat down in the oversized recliner. She took a moment to nestle Cole on her lap and then started reading.

Slowly, the tension began to drain out of her.

"C'mon, it'll be fun," Jordan Hall urged his best friend, Eric Logan.

He had to raise his voice in order to be heard over the rhythmic *whack* of the handball as it bounced against the far wall in the exclusive gym where they both had a membership. He and Eric were evenly matched and he had to concentrate in order not to lose the game. Not an easy feat when he was preoccupied with subtly laying the foundations of a plan.

He'd come up with the plan after getting off the phone with his mother. Elaine Hall had been bewailing the fact that, when Jennifer finally ventured out into the arena to which she had been born, it had to be for a deplorable bachelor auction.

"Of course it's for charity and that's all well and good," his mother had said to him, "but when is that sister of yours ever going to think about finding a suitable match for herself and finally settle down the way she's supposed to?"

It was the same refrain that his mother harassed him with. The same one, he knew, that Eric's mother, Leslie, occasionally played for him. Ordinarily, it would have gone in one ear and out the other, like a good many of the other one-way conversations his mother had had with him, except that this one had struck a chord. It had melded with one other piece of information in his brain that he was fairly certain no one else was privy to. He knew for a fact that Jenny had once had a major crush on Eric.

For all he knew, she still might.

In any event, the thought of the upcoming bachelor auction had led him to formulate an idea. Jenny was always about work and had completely forgotten how to play. In his less than humble opinion, his sister was in serious need of play. And he wanted to deliver it to her.

This was phase one.

"Fun," Eric snorted as he returned the serve, sending the ball slamming against the wall and then directly at Jordan. "Being paraded like a piece of meat in front of a room full of bored, aging society matrons with checkbooks is your idea of fun?"

"No, being paraded in front of the *daughters* of bored, aging society matrons with checkbooks of their own is fun," Jordan corrected, leaping up to reach the ball and send it shooting back toward the wall. "I've taken part in one of these auctions before. Trust me, it's for a very good cause and it fulfills your charity quota for at least six months."

A charity quota was the last thing Eric felt he needed to fill. "I gave at the office," he quipped, returning the serve. Despite the glove, his palm stung as he made contact.

They both knew his comeback was true. Everyone in Eric's family was dedicated, in varying degrees, to the concept of charity. Although Eric himself was seen as the carefree one in the family, a charming, desirable, eligible bachelor who was part of the vast Logan Corporation, a company that had long been near the top of the computer empire thanks to certain innovations and technology they'd developed, he was as serious about doing his part for charity as the rest, just not as visible about it. But Jordan knew that his friend had an affinity for the underdog and secretly did what he could to help things along.

That gave his best friend something in common with Jenny, Jordan thought. And he was counting on that to pave the way for an evening his little sister both deserved and wouldn't soon forget.

First, however, he needed to get Eric there.

"Give a little more," Jordan coaxed, his voice straining. He'd almost lost that last serve and struggled to recover it.

Sweat was pouring into Eric's sweatband. The terry cloth fabric felt as if it was glued to his forehead. He went long, captured the ball and sent it hurtling back to the wall.

"Why the sudden interest in my participation in this beefcake extravaganza?"

"My sister's chairing it." Jordan sneaked a side glance at Eric, but the latter's expression gave no indication that he even remembered Jenny. That could have just been his involvement in the game, since Eric always played to win. "And I thought I'd be a good big brother and recruit a few men for her. Besides," he said with a grin, "misery loves company."

With one mighty whack, Eric sent the ball flying over Jordan's shoulder. Triumph surged through his veins. The point was his.

Sports was the only field in which he allowed his natural sense of competition to emerge. God knew it wasn't at work. There his older brother Peter was the fair-haired boy, the company CEO to his department VP now that their father had retired. He'd become thoroughly convinced that Peter never slept. His older brother was there in the morning when Eric arrived at the office and remained there long after he went home.

Eric supposed that part of the deal was that Peter felt that he had to try twice as hard because he was adopted. The bottom line was that Peter achieved a tremendous amount and consequently left him looking as if he were standing still. If he was the insecure kind, this would have sent him running to the nearest therapist's couch, but he had a healthy sense of self that allowed him to view Peter's efforts as being good for the family, not reflecting badly on him.

If anything, it made him worry about his older brother. He felt as if Peter was allowing life to pass him by.

"Okay, I'll sign on. On one condition." He served the ball, then immediately braced himself for its return. "You talk Peter into it, too. He's the one who needs to get out, to unwind."

There was no hesitation on Jordan's part. "Sure,

Peter'd be a great addition to the stable." Jordan grinned, thinking of the serious man as he sent the ball flying. "Why don't you broach it with him first, though?"

"Me?" Eric echoed. Missing the ball, he muttered a curse under his breath. Then, with the ball out of play, he stopped for a second to catch his breath. "You're the pimp."

Picking up a bottle of water, Jordan stopped to drink before answering. "This isn't pimping." He wiped his forehead. "This is strictly aboveboard. You take the lady—"

"Who *paid* for my services," Eric was quick to point out.

"Who donated a great deal of money to a worthy charity for the pleasure of your company," Jordan corrected. Then he started again. "You take the lady out for the evening and show her a good time. That doesn't include warming any sheets." Jordan paused, knowing he couldn't come across like a choirboy without raising Eric's suspicions. "Unless, of course, you want to."

"What I want is never an issue. It's what the lady wants that counts," Eric told him with a touch of innocence that was a tad less than convincing.

Jordan was well aware of Eric's reputation as a heartthrob. "And you always make them want exactly what you want," he finished.

Eric took a deep breath, getting ready for another set. "Whatever you say."

Jordan bounced the ball once on the gym floor, then looked at Eric. "Then it's a yes?"

Eric shrugged. "Sure, why not? And I'll see about Peter." He gave Jordan a penetrating look. "You are in on this, right?"

"Wouldn't miss it." With that, Jordan served the ball with enthusiasm.

Phase one was complete, he thought. Now he needed to go on to phase two.

Two

Jenny threw back two extra-strength aspirins, washed them down with water and fervently hoped that they would live up to at least half of their advertising hype. Otherwise, she was ready to surrender now. Death by headache.

It was the kind of morning created by tiny devils gleefully working overtime in the bowels of hell. As far as she saw, there was no other plausible explanation why, when she was such a good person, everything that could go wrong today had. One right after the other.

Her alarm failed to go off, and for one of the few rare mornings of her life, she'd overslept. Then the toaster emitted flames instead of toast. That, luckily, had been handled by the fire extinguisher she'd had the presence of mind to keep in her cupboard. Cole's baby-sitter, a woman who thrived on punctuality and took pride in being early, was late. To top it off, her less than reliable car decided that it'd had enough of the distributor cap—the one her mechanic had put in just last month—and burned a hole through it.

Needless to say, that left her without a means of transportation to use in order to get to her downtown office. There wasn't even time to see about getting the evil car towed to her mechanic's shop. Telling herself she wasn't going to have a nervous breakdown, she just left the vehicle parked in the carport and hurried back to her apartment to call a taxi.

When she'd arrived at her office, there were a pile of messages already on her desk, threatening to breed if left unread. And her appointments were backing up.

On mornings like this that life of leisure her mother kept advocating began to sound awfully tempting.

Still waiting for the aspirins to kick in and do their magic, Jenny was only one third through her pile of messages and in between the battalion of clients when the secretary she shared with the other attorneys who made up Advocate Aid, Inc.—a title she'd come up with because it was short and to the point, unlike her life—called out across the communal space they all shared.

"Line three's for you, Jenny."

Jenny cringed. She felt as if an anvil had just been dropped on top of her head. There was such a thing as physically and mentally reaching a limit and she had well surpassed hers. She'd stayed up last night to work on the Ortiz case, but then one of Cole's nightmares had brought her rushing to his side. She'd remained there, consoling him, until he'd fallen asleep.

Unfortunately, so had she.

Slumbering in Cole's undersized junior bed while assuming a position made popular by early Christian martyrs had given her a phenomenal crick in her neck. One that refused to go away even when bombarded with an extra three minutes worth of hot water in the shower.

She rubbed it now, telling herself that this, too, shall pass, as she called back, "Tell them I died."

"Really?"

She'd forgotten that Betty was a woman who took you at your word. Literally. She was completely devoid of any sense of humor, droll or otherwise.

"No," Jenny sighed, "not really."

Rotating her neck from side to side, she picked up the receiver. As she placed it to her ear, Jenny struggled with the sinking feeling that she was going to regret not sticking to her original instruction.

Trying to sound as cheerful as she could under the circumstances, she said, "Hello, this is Jennifer Hall."

"Mother called me last night."

Tension temporarily slid out of her body as she recognized her brother's voice. Jordan represented a moment's respite from her otherwise miserable day. "My condolences."

She heard him chuckle before he continued. "She said that you were chairing that fund-raising bachelor auction again."

Undoubtedly her mother had probably said a lot of other things, as well, about the situation, bemoaning the fact that once again, the daughter she'd raised for great things and adoring men was once more on the sidelines. Camille in her deathbed scene definitely had nothing on her mother. Mingling amid men had always come easy for her mother. The woman didn't understand that not everyone was granted that gift.

"Those that can, do. Those that can't, auction," Jenny replied glibly.

Her brother surprised her with the serious note in his voice. "Don't knock yourself down, Jenny. The only reason you're not out there every night is because you choose not to be."

"Right." Never mind the fact that she was plain, she thought, and that no one without some grievance to file would give her the time of day, much less the time of her life.

The natives along the wall were getting restless and she had several people to see before she could leave for court. "Listen, Jordy, I'd love to talk, but—"

He got to the crux of his call, or at least, the beginning of it. "I've called to volunteer my services for the auction."

Again she was surprised. She scribbled her brother's name on the side of her blotter with a note about the bachelor auction. One thing that went right today. Maybe it would start a trend.

"Fantastic, Jordy. This means I don't have to badger you." Although she was only going to turn to him if she couldn't get anyone else. She knew that this was not high on Jordan's list of favorite things to do.

"No, but you might have to do a little persuading with the two other candidates I lined up for you."

That stopped her cold. "Oh?"

Intrigued, she turned her swivel chair away from the lineup against the far wall. She didn't exactly have time for this now, but she was going to have to make time later. The auction was less than two weeks away and she still needed more bodies to fill the quota. Especially since Emerson Davis just dropped out due to a sudden marriage that no one but the bartender who'd kept refilling Emerson's glass in the Vegas club saw coming.

Still, she knew when to be cautious. "Exactly who did you 'line up' for me?"

"Peter Logan and his brother." Peter Logan had two brothers as well as two sisters. Jordan paused significantly, as if waiting for a drumroll, before he finally said, "Eric."

Eric.

Beautiful Eric.

Eric with the soulful brown eyes and thick, luscious brown hair. Eric who still, after all these years, popped up in her dreams just often enough to remind her that she had never quite gotten over that crush she'd had on him all those years ago.

Everyone had an impossible dream. Eric was hers. But dreams, Jenny had learned, did not arbitrarily come true, especially if you did nothing to make them come true. And she, un-swanlike as she was, had kept her distance from Eric Logan. The man was accustomed to drop-dead gorgeous women, a label she knew in her heart would never be applied to her, not even by a myopic, tenderhearted man.

She felt herself growing warm at the mere sound of Eric's name. She really hoped that a blush wasn't working its way up her neck to her face, although it probably was, if that look from the man seated against the wall, waiting to speak to her, was any indication.

"Jenny? Are you there?" Jordan asked as the silence stretched out between them.

She cleared her throat, silently calling herself a dunce. "You, um, you talked to them?"

"I talked to Peter. He suggested Eric join us, and thought that an appeal from you might cinch the deal."

"Appeal to Eric," she repeated as if in a trance.

"You might."

And then she laughed. "Yeah, right."

The next moment, she came to her senses and realized she'd taken that in the wrong context. God knew she would have given her right arm to appeal to Eric, but she wasn't his type. She had far more of a chance of winning the Kentucky Derby than she had of appealing to Eric.

There was silence again and she was quick to remedy it. "You're his best friend, Jordan. You talk to him."

"Can't."

"Why?"

"Because, as his best friend, Eric wouldn't be uncomfortable saying no to me. But he won't say no to you. Especially since his parents have donated a considerable amount of money to your cause as well as to the Children's Connection," he told her, mentioning the name of the adoption organization associated with both Portland General Hospital and PAN itself. "He just needs a little convincing."

She knew all about the Logans' generosity, as well as what Eric did and didn't do. She made it a point to keep tabs on him, even if he was completely unattainable. "And you think I can do that."

"Hey, you're the chairlady. I can't do all your work for you. Besides, you're the one who can argue the ears off an Indian Elephant."

She supposed that was a compliment, although she'd had better. "Lovely image."

"You'll find him at Logan Corporation. I know he's free this afternoon about one." Jordan paused. "He's expecting you."

She was due in court by three o'clock. That gave her a small margin of time if she juggled it right and had lunch at her desk.

So what else was new?

Jenny felt her heart hammering as she echoed incredulously, "He's expecting me?"

"Uh-huh. I told Eric that you might drop by to try to convince him to jump on the bandwagon, so to speak."

Jenny felt her mouth becoming completely dry. That was because all the moisture in her body had suddenly rerouted itself straight to her hands and then condensed there.

She heard herself saying with more than a little disbelief, "Then I guess one o'clock it is."

"Great. Talk to you about the details later."

She wasn't sure if her brother was referring to the details involved in his taking part in the auction, or the details of what was probably going to prove to be her latest mortifying experience, but she didn't have the opportunity to ask. Jordan had hung up.

Gripping both sides of the desk, she rose from behind it on shaky legs that had suddenly been rented out to someone else. In a gait she knew had to approximate that of Frankenstein's monster as he took his first unattended steps, she began to cross to the hall.

"Hey, your next appointment is here," Betty hissed to her as Jenny strode past the younger woman's cluttered desk.

Jenny didn't even spare Betty a look. She couldn't. Moving her head to the left or right might carry dangerous consequences with it.

"Tell them I'll be right back."

Getting accustomed to her new wooden legs, Jenny quickened her steps as she hurried to the bathroom. To throw up.

For a second after she exited the cab, Jenny stood on the curb, looking up at the tall edifice before her. The building that was owned by and housed the Logan Corporation. With effort, she gathered together the last drops of her courage. She needed all the help she could get.

Despite her last appointment running over, she'd made it to the Logan Corporation building with a few minutes to spare.

All the way over to the shining thirty-story edifice she had practiced what she was going to say to Eric once she was alone with him. But, unlike when she was preparing to deliver summations in court, no amount of rehearsal seemed to improve her performance. The moment she went through her arguments, they melted from her brain like lone snowflakes out on a June sidewalk.

He was just a man, she told herself as she rode up the elevator to his floor. Two legs, two arms, one body in between to hold the limbs together. Beneath his tanned skin he had the same skeletal structure as millions of other men.

But oh, that skin, Jenny caught herself thinking. And growing warmer.

This thinking was going to get her nowhere. Worse, if she wasn't careful, it would lose the auction a potential and incredibly desirable bachelor. The fewer bachelors, the less money would be raised. Any fool could see that having Eric Logan on the block would raise the organization a very pretty penny.

There were no two ways about it. She had to think of him as just another body.

Focus, focus, she ordered herself as she stepped off the elevator and walked down the hallway to the inner sanctum that was the gateway to his office.

His office lay just behind the massive double doors. As the VP of Marketing & Sales for the Logan Corporation, Eric occupied an impressive suite. She had no doubts that the entire staff of Advocate Aid, Inc. could easily fit into it with room to spare, desks and all.

She presented herself to the keeper of the gate. "I'm Jennifer Hall. Mr. Logan is expecting me."

Unlike Betty, who came to work in jeans that had seen a better century, the woman she addressed looked as if she had been forged out of a mold that was labeled: Perfect Secretary.

The woman smiled distantly but politely, then checked a list before her.

"Yes, he is," she replied coolly. "If you'll come this way." Rising to her feet, the secretary led the way back. She knocked on the door, then turned the knob, opening the door just wide enough to allow Jenny to slip through. "Ms. Hall to see you, sir."

Nodding her thanks to the woman, Jenny crossed the threshold. When the door closed again behind her, Jenny concentrated on not sinking to the floor in a heap.

She looked like the personification of efficiency, Eric thought as he rose to his feet to greet Jenny. Every light brown hair was pulled back and in place, except for one wayward wisp at her right temple that seemed to have rebelliously disengaged itself from the rest.

It made her look more human, he thought, his eyes sweeping over the rest of her. Jordan's sister was wearing a light gray suit that appeared just large enough to hide her figure.

Was there a figure beneath all that, or was she shapeless?

Didn't matter one way or another. He reminded himself that this was his best friend's sister and not another conquest to be won over. This was strictly business, not pleasure. If anything, he was doing a favor for a friend. A friend to whom he'd ultimately lost a handball game to yesterday.

"Sit down." He gestured toward the comfortable chair before his desk.

"Thank you for seeing me."

The words were uttered slowly, distinctly. She wasn't enunciating so much as trying to work around a tongue that felt as if it had swollen to three times its normal size. Sitting, she leaned her briefcase against the back of the desk and placed her hands on either armrest, praying she wouldn't leave damp streaks on them. Her palms felt as if they were more than one half water.

Taking a deep breath, she launched into her campaign, fervently hoping she wouldn't sound like a blithering idiot to him.

"I realize that your time is precious, Eric—" She could call him Eric, couldn't she? After all, they did go way back, technically. "But this is a very worthy cause." Her palms grew damper, her speech rate increased. "Since 1989, PAN—that's the Parent Adoption Network—has been able to help—"

Was she trying to convince him? he wondered. He was under the impression, after talking to Jordan, that this was a done deal. "Yes."

The single word pulled her up short. She felt like someone slamming on the brake and skidding back and forth along the road, trying not to hit something. "Yes?"

Was there something he wasn't getting? Or had Jordan failed to tell her that he had agreed to this? "Yes, I'll be part of the bachelor auction. That's what you were leading up to, wasn't it?"

"Yes." She blew out a breath, her mind a sudden blank with nothing available in the immediate area with which to fill it. She flushed. "Wow, that certainly takes the wind out of my sails."

He found pink was an appealing color on her. Maybe she wasn't quite as plain as how she first came across. Jenny did have beautiful blue eyes. "Why? Didn't you want me to say yes?"

"Yes." She liked the sound of that word in her ear, the taste of it on her tongue. Yes... There were so many scenarios she wanted Eric and herself to agree on....

Yanking herself out of her mental revelry, she tried to backtrack. She wasn't going to suffer death by headache today. No, if she was going to die today, it was going to be death by sheer idiocy. "I mean, I've been looking for the right words to persuade you, practicing speeches." Because Eric was looking at her so intently, she flushed again. She tried not to contemplate what was going through his mind. "The cabby must have thought I was crazy."

"Cabby?"

Jenny nodded. "I had to take a cab to get here. Actually, I had to take a cab to get anywhere today. My car died." She felt her tongue tangling more and more and waved a hand at her words. She'd gone off on a tangent again. It was what happened when her brain wasn't operating properly. "Never mind, you don't want to hear about that."

Eric smiled at her. Jenny found her knees dissolving like sugar cubes in a hot cup of coffee. Any second now she was going to turn into a complete puddle.

"I've been subjected to worse things," he confided. Glancing over at his day planner, Eric made a decision. "Why don't we grab a cup of coffee somewhere and talk over exactly what you want me to do?"

Oh, if you only knew. Jenny grabbed her thoughts before they could bolt from the corral and go off running.

This was a bad idea, she thought.

Her confidence didn't come into play in this arena the way it did when she was in the courtroom. There she was completely prepared, knew her case's strengths, its weaknesses. Here, the only weakness she was acutely aware of was her own.

This wasn't about her, Jenny upbraided herself. This was about charity. She had to stop thinking like an adolescent and start thinking and behaving like the mature twenty-six-year-old woman she was. A twenty-six-year-old woman who was a damn good attorney and had graduated at the top of her class within a highly competitive academic forum.

A twenty-six-year old woman-slash-attorney who was turning into mush while looking up into warm chocolate-brown eyes that reminded her of her favorite pudding.

Enough.

Exercising tremendous self-control, Jenny forced herself to think practically, not an easy matter under the circumstances. She had to be in court by three, which meant she needed to be inside a cab by two-fifteen. That in turn meant calling a cab by one forty-five. Since it was a little after one o'clock now, that gave her approximately forty-five minutes.

Forty-five minutes to bask in Eric Logan's smile and try very, very hard not to behave like a living brain donor. It was a challenge.

"Sounds good to me." She slowly peeled the words off the roof of her mouth one by one.

The next moment, Jenny looked away from the even wider smile that was now gracing Eric's lips. She had to. She knew she wasn't about to regain the use of her knees any other way.

Three

The coffee shop turned out to be just around the corner from the Logan Corporation. There were tables outside the shop for those who felt like facing the brisk early December afternoon. In deference to the weather, Eric selected one inside for them. It was close to the window so that they still had a good view of all the foot traffic on the busy thoroughfare.

Eric waited until they were both seated and facing each other across a small, round oak table before he said anything beyond asking her what kind of coffee she felt like having.

He watched her take a delicate sip. Jordan's sister had nice features, he decided, but someone needed to introduce her to makeup.

Still, he knew a great many women who, deprived of their paints, powders and brushes, looked far less attractive than Jenny did. There was something to be said for that.

"So, is this what you do?" Eric asked.

With Eric so close, at times brushing against her in this crowd, it was all Jenny could do to focus on what he was saying, to put one foot in front of the other and keep walking. Thinking was out of the question, so she hit on the first thing that came to her mind.

"You mean badger men?"

He laughed and though it was dangerous to her newly returning sanity, she allowed herself to absorb the rich sound and bask in it for a moment before, once again, reminding herself that this was not about her long-standing infatuation with Eric, it was about the charity.

Ah, but charity begins at home, a tiny voice whispered, *and wouldn't you like to take him home?*

Jenny shifted in her seat, as if to physically get away from the thought that neatly tucked itself under the heading of impossible dreams.

"No," Eric said, "I meant fund-raising."

Holding her gaily decorated cup in both hands, she stared into the light chocolate liquid, making a deliberate effort to avoid his eyes. If she looked into them, she knew she could easily get lost. And without a lifeline or compass to guide her, she might never be able to find her way back.

"No," she replied, raising her voice above the murmuring din. "I'm an attorney."

Eric cocked his head and looked at her, as if absorbing the information and trying to apply it to her. "Really."

It sounded as if it was half a question, half a statement uttered in disbelief. Obviously her big brother didn't talk to Eric about her. Not that she would have expected him to, she supposed. When handsome men in their prime got together, siblings were probably the last things they talked about.

From some automatic pilot region that was usually tapped into only when her mother was around, Jenny felt her backbone stiffening.

"Yes, really."

She saw amusement curving his mouth. Did he find lawyers amusing, or just the idea of her being one?

"Which firm?" he asked.

"Advocate Aid, Inc." There was a touch of pride in her voice as she told him. They were an incredibly small group, numbering four now that Russell had bailed on them. But they were a proud group nonetheless.

Eric really hadn't expected that. He'd thought that Jennifer's father's connections would have placed her in some highbrow law firm, the way they had Jordan. He tried picturing her in less than affluent surroundings and came up short.

"Why?"

Jenny's back became ramrod straight. This she

was accustomed to. Being challenged. For a moment, she forgot that a glance from Eric Logan's soft brown eyes could melt steel pins at a hundred paces. Her protective nature came out, the same nature that allowed her to champion so many of the championless people who came her way, looking upon her as their last chance.

"Because they need someone on their side a lot more than the people who come to Jordan's firm do."

Eric wondered if this was something she truly believed in, or just something she felt she should be giving lip service to. So many men and women involved in charities only did so by remote control. They kept their hearts completely out of the affair.

Because the noise level was rising, he leaned forward across the table. "So you're saying the poor need more justice than the rich?"

It felt as if his face was inches from hers. She could feel his breath along her skin. Could feel the inside of her body coiling, ready to spring. Not that she ever would. She was too terrified to make a move.

It took her a second to find her voice. "No, I'm saying the poor are just as much entitled to it as the rich and because they're poor, they don't get it."

His eyes held hers. She had nice eyes, he thought. Sincere eyes. He began to believe her. Or at least believe that she believed herself. "Except for you."

He was smiling again. Was that indulgence? Gas? Or something more meaningful?

She struggled not to sink into his expression. "I'm not the Lone Crusader here. There are others, although not nearly enough." The sigh escaped her before she realized it had been hovering in the wings.

The last time he'd heard anyone sigh like that, it was the man next to him at the blackjack table. The man had lost ten thousand dollars at a single turn of the cards. "That sounded pretty intense. Care to elaborate?"

Before she knew it, Jenny found herself doing just that.

Eric, she realized, had the ability to draw words out of her despite the fact that they had to get past a blank mind and a thick tongue. She concluded that the man was nothing short of a magician. The kind who pulled on a single scarf only to draw out another and another while the audience looked on in awe.

But maybe he was just being polite. She didn't want to bore him with details. "It's just gotten a little harder since Russell left."

"Russell?"

She nodded. Since he hadn't yawned or had his attention drawn away by the voluptuous redhead who was unabashedly staring at him from across the room, Jenny continued.

"Russell Riley. He was one of the founders of Advocate Aid, Inc." Russell had been the one to recruit her, straight out of law school. The ink hadn't dried yet on her diploma when he'd told her about the fledgling law firm that he and his friends had put together so that they could practice "real" law as he'd put it. "He just up and quit one day."

A wry smile played on her lips as she recalled the scene in her head. Recalled progressing from guarded amusement when she thought Russell was kidding, to disbelief, to utter sorrow. And finally to anger because he was deserting them after getting her so caught up in the concept.

"He said he'd had enough of tilting at windmills. That the windmills had won and he was taking an offer from a firm that could actually help him pay his bills at the end of the month." She supposed she couldn't fault the man. After all, she had never been in that position herself. Maybe she would have thought differently if it was a matter of choosing between paying her rent and eating that week.

Finished with his espresso, Eric toyed with the empty cup, his eyes on her. "Don't you ever feel that way?"

"My bills are paid at the end of the month." At times, the admission almost embarrassed her. It was what separated her from the people she was trying to help. They were poor and she was far from it, even if she didn't take a cent from her parents. That was because of the inheritance. "I had a very generous grandmother who left me more than enough money in her will."

Eric shook his head. One strand of brown hair fell into his eyes and she had to curve her fingers into her palms to keep from reaching out and sweeping the strand back into place. "No, I meant tired of tilting at windmills."

She smiled. "Sometimes." She was unaware that exhilaration entered her voice. But he wasn't. "But then, those wonderful times when the windmills lose—and they do lose—make it all worth it. So does the expression on the face of my client, a person who thought no one cared and that he was doomed to be the one that everyone else stepped on." Forgetting who she was talking to for a moment, she warmed to her subject, to her unending quest. "I deal in hope and there's no greater high than to see it actually take root and spread."

She realized that he'd gotten quiet. Not bored, just quiet. He was looking at her as if she was saying something he was actually interested in.

Also his gift, she thought.

She'd heard women say that Eric Logan could instantly make them feel as if they were the only ones in a room crowded with people. It was true. The coffee shop he'd brought her to was fairly full with a post-lunch crowd milking the last minutes of their break before returning to whatever they had to return to. She'd seen more than one woman look Eric's way as they walked past table after full table. Attractive women sitting across from attractive men.

But then, Eric was in a class all his own. He had a certain something. Magnetism, she thought it was called.

It could have been called Oscar for all she knew, Jenny thought. The only thing she was certain of was that it still had a deep effect on her.

He was smiling at her, really smiling. Not indulgently, the way a person did when they pasted on a smile and counted off the minutes until someone was through talking to them, but genuinely.

Or was that only wishful thinking on her part? "What?" she finally asked.

Eric sobered ever so slightly. He didn't want her thinking he was laughing at her. "It's just that Jordan never mentioned any of this. The only time he talked about you was to say you were chairing some charitable event. I had no idea Jordan's little sister had turned into Joan of Arc."

Self-consciousness returned in droves. Once again she was that little girl in the living room with two left shoes on. It had taken her years to live that down. Her mother kept it in her arsenal, ready to pull out at a moment's notice.

"Did I just sound too pompous?"

He read her expression quickly and with regret. In his opinion, there weren't enough true do-gooders in the world. "I'm sorry, I didn't mean to make it sound as if I was poking fun at you, I was just impressed. My parents would have been, too. They believe very strongly in the concept of giving back."

A light turned on inside of her, burning brightly. He was impressed. Eric Logan was impressed with her. Never mind that it was for something she did as routinely as breathing, he'd taken notice of her. She felt lighter than air.

"It's not so much a matter of giving back as it is just trying to balance the odds." She caught her lower lip between her teeth. "I'm sorry, I didn't mean to go off on a tangent like that."

"It wasn't a tangent," Eric protested. "As I remember, I asked you a question."

She tried not to flush and mentally upbraided herself for her reaction when she did.

What was it about the way the man spoke, looked, hell, *breathed,* that negated all her schooling, all her thoughts, everything inside her head and gave her the IQ of a dull button?

"The question you should be asking is about the fund-raiser."

Then, as if he had done just that, Jenny went on to give him the date, time and location of the affair. The Portland Hilton had graciously donated one of their larger ballrooms for the evening in exchange for the publicity the fund-raiser was guaranteed to generate in the local newspapers. She'd already made a point to release the story to the *Herald* and the *Tribune,* making sure there would be follow-ups on the night of the event. Sleep these days came at a high premium.

She watched Eric jot down the information and held her breath as he went through his PalmPilot and made sure he had no conflicting engagement. To her relief and minor disbelief, he didn't.

So far, so good.

"I'll need you there at least half an hour before the auction starts," she told him as he closed his Palm-Pilot and tucked it away into the breast pocket of his Armani jacket.

"Will you, now?"

Jenny knew the teasing words were uttered just in fun, but she felt them slide down her spine like the warm, caressing fingers of a lover. Or what she imagined the warm, caressing fingers of a lover would feel like, never having had the firsthand experience herself.

It took effort not to shiver as the sensation danced through her.

From some unknown source, she discovered an iota of saliva and husbanded it before swallowing to relieve a throat that was suddenly so parched, it made the Mojave Desert look like a rain forest.

"I mean we need you there earlier so we can go over the order you'll all be in and what you want me to say when I introduce you to the bidders."

"I have to write my own intro?" He hadn't thought of that. Listing his accomplishments wasn't something he was accustomed to.

Jenny thought of last year. A great many of the men who were auctioned off had very clear ideas about what she should say about them before the bidding began. "A lot of the bachelors like doing that."

Eric shrugged carelessly. "Why don't you take

care of that?" he suggested. In his estimation, she looked a little stunned. "Say anything you want to say."

How about *"I love you"*?

Jenny blinked with a jolt, as startled by the unbidden thought as she knew he would have been had she said it out loud.

Eric interpreted her reaction to be to his words, not some thought that had suddenly occurred to her. "What, no good?"

She tried to suck in a breath as covertly as possible. "No, that'll be fine. I think I know enough about you to make an intelligent presentation." Striving to look anywhere but at his face, she glanced down at her wrist. And saw her watch. The numbers registered and she groaned. "Oh, God."

"What's wrong?"

She looked up at him, fighting a growing panic. She was going to be late. This was just par for today. "It's two o'clock."

"And just what time did your fairy godmother tell you to be back?" he teased. He didn't exactly know why, but everything about Jenny made him think of Cinderella. "Do your clothes start disappearing now, changing into tatters?"

With her thoughts scattering in two directions at once, his words made no sense to her. She absolutely hated being late. She pictured poor Miguel and his family waiting for her in the long courthouse hallway, thinking that she had deserted them. "What?"

She began rummaging through her purse for her cell phone, praying that the battery hadn't been struck dead by some fluke of nature. "No. I mean, I'm due in court at three."

Taking her wrist, he turned it slightly so he could read the face on her watch, as well. "That still gives you an hour."

She could feel her skin throbbing where his thumb and forefinger had touched it. "Yes, but I need to call a cab and if there's traffic—"

He placed his hand over hers to curtail the stream of words he saw coming. Unable to quite read it, Eric found himself curious about the look that leaped into her eyes.

"Why don't I drive you to court?"

The casual offer had air rushing out of her lungs like helium from a punctured balloon. "What?"

Was it his imagination, or did she look flustered? "Why don't I drive you to court?" he repeated, then grinned. "That would solve your problem, wouldn't it?"

All but for the lobotomy his smile was threatening to perform on her brain. She ran the tip of her dry tongue along her drier lips.

"Don't you have to get back to the office?" she asked hoarsely.

It had been a full, if unproductive morning. "All of today's crises have been safely averted," he informed her. "And if a new one crops up, Peter'll handle it." He thought of his older brother, shoulder to the wheel, nose to the grindstone. His father couldn't have asked for a better son to run the company if he had had him made to order. "Peter always handles it."

Was that a note of sibling rivalry she detected? No, if that were the case, then Eric would have been anxious to get back into the arena. It was more as if he was acknowledging the lines that had been drawn.

"Peter's very conscientious." It wasn't really a guess. Jordan had told her as much.

"That he is," Eric agreed. "To a fault." He remembered the way Jenny had come into his office, armed with rhetoric he hadn't allowed her to unleash. "He's the one you may have to talk into doing this auction."

She finished her coffee and crumpled her cup. It was a nervous habit. "Jordan's done handling that for me."

He nodded, taking in the information. "Wise choice. Jordan can talk the sun into not setting." His eyes shifted to her face. Had he just unintentionally insulted her? "No offense to you intended."

She didn't follow him. "Offense?"

"I didn't mean you couldn't persuade Peter if you wanted to. I'm sure you can be very persuasive if you want to be."

There it was again, that thousand-watt smile. Even when it was turned down a notch, it completely undid her.

Talk, damn it, Jenny, talk. Answer the man.

She couldn't just continue to sit here and blush

like some single-celled idiot, she told herself. She said the only thing she truthfully could. "I win more cases than I lose."

It took him a second to remember she was a lawyer. "You mean in court."

Was he trying to tell her that it didn't work that way in the world beyond the hallowed halls of justice? "Yes, but—"

He wasn't completely sure why, but he suddenly had a yen to see her in action for himself. "Would you mind if I came with you?"

"Where?" And then she realized what he was saying. Her eyes widened in surprise and unease. "You mean *into* court?"

He laughed at her expression. "I don't think the bailiff will let me listen against the door." And then he saw a look that was akin to horror cross her face. "Unless having me there will throw you a curve," he qualified. "I wouldn't want you jeopardizing the case just because I've decided to go touring—"

Damn it, get a hold of yourself before he thinks you're some weak-kneed loon.

Never mind that she was.

There was absolutely no reason for her heart to suddenly start pounding like this, not unless she was having a genuine heart attack. *C'mon, c'mon, you're made of sterner stuff than this.*

A few weeks ago, she'd argued in front of a judge who routinely spit nails and chewed up lawyers for a snack. And she'd won. If she could do that, certainly she could survive having the most gorgeous man in God's creation sitting in her courtroom, watching her plead a case, she reasoned.

If she kept Miguel's face uppermost in her mind, she'd be all right, she told herself. And, after all, this was about what amounted to the rest of a man's life. If she lost, the quality of that life promised to be unbearably low. It was up to her to raise it, to show Miguel Ortiz that not everyone was going to ignore him and the plight he found himself in.

Taking a breath, she found her voice. "No, having you there won't jeopardize the case." She jumped on the first excuse that came to her. "I just thought that you might be bored."

Eric looked at her, that same sensual smile she knew she was never going to become immune to spreading over his generous lips.

"I have a feeling that boredom isn't going to enter into the picture."

Taking her elbow, he escorted her from the now crowded coffee shop and out onto the curb. Jenny felt as if she was floating and wondered if her feet actually touched the pavement.

They headed back to Logan Corporation's building and its underground parking where his Ferrari was patiently waiting. He aimed his key ring at it and disarmed the alarm. "How strong is your case?"

"Very strong."

She didn't add that it was because of her endless digging that the case had shaped up the way it had.

Every single spare moment after hours that wasn't earmarked for Cole had been spent interviewing people, gathering information and compiling a case against both the surgeon, Dr. Wilson Turner, and the hospital that had neglected to police the derelict physician.

Because of her tireless efforts, she'd discovered that many in the tight Portland medical community thought Turner was a disaster waiting to happen.

And he had happened to Miguel Ortiz.

"Then this should be interesting," Eric told her as he held the passenger side door open for her.

What would be interesting, she thought as she got into the vehicle, was whether or not she still remembered how to speak once they finally arrived at the courthouse.

Exposure to the virus, she thought, slanting a glance toward Eric as he started up the car, did not breed immunity.

It only intensified the fever.

Four

Eric negotiated through the early-afternoon traffic in the same manner he negotiated through life, skillfully slipping in and out of any available space and making good time. They made it to the courthouse with ten minutes to spare.

"Jordan didn't tell me you drove on the NASCAR circuit," Jenny commented as she got out.

He flashed her what she'd come to think of as a million-dollar grin.

"Just taking advantage of the opportunities, Jen." He aimed his key ring at the vehicle, arming the security device. It squeaked in response. "You did want to get here on time, right?"

Jen. He'd called her Jen. No one called her Jen.

It made her feel impossibly sophisticated and on top of things.

For about a second and a half, until he took her arm and escorted her to the electronic courthouse doors.

Having him within ten feet of her did some very strange things to her synapses. Having him touch her, even through clothing, all but short-circuited them. Remembering her name was a challenge.

"It's on the second floor," she told him as she held her briefcase open for the guard to check.

They took the escalator up because it was faster than waiting for an elevator. She was acutely aware that he was standing on the step behind her. The fragrance of his cologne made her grab onto her mind before it took off on the wings of fantasy.

Miguel Ortiz and his wife and daughter were already waiting for her. Jenny saw the refurbished wheelchair she'd managed to procure for the man, replacing the wobbly secondhand one he'd been using when he'd first brought the case to her.

The surgeon they were suing had put Miguel in that chair. Permanently.

It had begun as a simple case of a man being injured at his place of work. Something that happened every day somewhere in the country and was usually temporary. Working at the loading dock of one of the country's more well-known overnight shipping companies, Miguel had hurt his back and neck on the job. After three months of futile visits to various HMO physicians, Miguel was referred to Dr. Wilson Turner, a noted orthopedic surgeon who had been with the HMO only a year. At the time, no one had known that Turner had lost his license in another state. Turner told Miguel that he needed a simple operation to correct the disc problem. One the surgeon had assured Miguel he could do with his eyes shut.

Which was almost the way he'd performed the surgery. It was later discovered that Turner had managed to chip the bone, lodging a sliver into Miguel's spine. Miguel had emerged from the operation unable to move either one of his legs and was in terrible agony every single moment he was awake.

It took several more operations, done by someone who Miguel's insurance deemed to be "outside the system" to get him to where his pain was bearable. But there was no reversing the ultimate damage done as a result of Turner's incompetence. Miguel was disabled.

Stopping before the threesome, Jenny greeted each one warmly.

Alma Ortiz, Miguel's sixteen-year-old daughter, took a deep breath, as if bracing herself for the afternoon that lay before them. "This is pretty much it, isn't it?"

There had been investigations, miles of paperwork and scores of interviews. She'd flown to Utah to get firsthand information about the surgeon's license being revoked and paid for the flight out of her own pocket. And now they were down to the wire.

"Yes, it is. Unless they turn us down," she qualified. Jenny saw the look of disappointment descending over the girl's face. "But then we have several ways to go." She slipped her arm around the girl's slim shoulders, giving her a quick hug. "I'm not giving up until your dad's set for life, okay?" She looked at the couple before her, humbled by the trust she saw there.

Rosa Ortiz's command of the English language was limited, far more so than her husband's. But both reacted to the confident look in Jenny's eyes. They nodded in response.

And then, curiously, they shifted their gaze to just beyond her shoulder.

Jenny suddenly realized that for a few moments there, she'd completely forgotten that Eric was with her. Embarrassed, she turned toward him.

"Eric, this is Mr. and Mrs. Ortiz," she gestured toward the couple, "and their daughter, Alma. This is Eric Logan."

Eric leaned forward, first shaking Miguel's hand and then that of his wife and daughter.

Miguel's dark eyes shifted from Jenny's face to Eric's and then back again. He raised a dark eyebrow. *"Su novio?"*

At the speed of light, Jenny's complexion turned from white to a deep pink. "No, no," she uttered emphatically, afraid that Eric understood Spanish. "Eric's just a friend."

Unconsciously resting his hand on her waist, Eric leaned into her. He liked the shade of pink he saw creeping up her cheeks again. Pretending he didn't speak Spanish, he asked, "What did he just ask?"

Stop touching me, Eric. I can't think if you're touching me.

"I asked her if you were her intended," Miguel replied. Then, obviously not satisfied with the word he'd used, he looked at his daughter for help.

"Fiancé," Alma supplied.

The word did nothing to help Jenny's skin tone return to normal.

Taking pity on her, Eric explained, "I'm her brother's best friend." Then he leaned over and whispered into Jenny's ear, "Pink looks good on you."

His warm breath sizzled against her skin. Her embarrassment deepened.

Jenny struggled to focus, to somehow shut out Eric's presence. To shut out the feel of his breath on her skin, his whisper in her ear. It was like trying to suck up smoke with a vacuum cleaner.

But she had to manage it somehow. They were down to the wire here. This was about all the marbles and she needed a clear head.

She'd already turned down an out-of-court offer, which she considered too low. The Ortizes were willing to go along with her instincts and her determination. They had faith in her. Faith she was terrified of disappointing.

The double doors to her left opened.

A tall, imposing balding bailiff stood in the space between the outer courtroom doors and the inner ones.

His expression was dour. She hoped it wasn't an omen.

The man didn't say anything, allowing his presence to say it all.

"Okay, this is it. Showtime, people." Pausing, Jenny waited for the couple and their daughter to go into the courtroom first.

"Knock 'em dead," Eric whispered to her.

An army of goose bumps marched up and down her arms, then went single file down her spine.

"That's the general idea," she told him, trying hard to appear as nonchalant as the women who populated his world.

A noise on the far end of the hall caught her attention. The army of lawyers retained by Mercy General Hospital was walking toward them.

Toward her.

The knot in her stomach simultaneously tightened and got bigger.

"Looks a little like the scene from *Gunfight at the O.K. Corral,* doesn't it?" Eric observed, looking at the five men and one woman coming their way.

Jenny ran the tip of her tongue along her lips. "The good guys won that one," she murmured, fervently praying that history would repeat itself.

With that, she squared her shoulders and followed the Ortiz family into the courtroom.

It was like watching another person entirely.

If Jennifer Hall seemed a little unsure of herself,

a little disorganized or muddled when she'd first spoken to him in his office, the face she put on in front of the judge and the opposing attorneys was nothing short of supremely confident, supremely prepared. As she spoke, weaving point into salient point, she held the jury in the palm of her hand.

Eric found himself thinking that if he ever needed someone to represent him, he would more readily turn to her rather than the slew of corporate lawyers Logan Corporation employed.

As he observed her, the thought struck him that perhaps Jenny might welcome a job change. He knew his father had always approved of people who were at the top of their game and she would be a welcome addition to their stable of topflight lawyers. She'd be fresh, young blood. Since she was involved in legal aid, he knew that Jenny had to be up on many facets of the law.

He was well aware that corporate law wasn't nearly the dynamic battlefield that this might be, but it was vital to the continuation of the Logan Corporation.

He made a mental note to broach the subject to her, feel her out, maybe even just before the auction. For all he knew, despite her declaration that she liked tilting at windmills, she might secretly be growing tired of the battles.

At some point, he thought, unconsciously quoting his mother, people needed to stop fighting and settle back to enjoy the finer things in life.

Eric glanced at his watch. He'd had no idea that so much time had gone by. Heaven knew that he'd remained here far longer than he had initially intended. He was only going to stop for a moment, maybe add a little silent mental support, but he'd been captured by her style right from the start.

And now, if he didn't hurry, he was going to be late for his own meeting. And after that, there was Mona.

Waiting until Jenny's back was to him again, Eric slipped silently out of the courtroom. Once outside the second set of double doors, he hurried to the escalator, taking the metal steps down two at a time.

He wondered how the vivacious redhead he'd been seeing for the last three or four weeks would take the fact that he had allowed himself to be signed up for a bachelor auction. Probably not all that well.

Not that it had any bearing on his ultimate decision. She was already getting a little too clingy for his tastes and he never entered a relationship with the thought of being there for the long haul.

The best he could do were short ones.

Taking a deep breath, Jenny faced the jury that had sat and listened to the evidence she'd so carefully gathered over these last few months.

The key evidence was testimony from an operating room nurse and the surgeon who had assisted Turner. The latter had been deemed by the court as a hostile witness, unwilling to be there, but just as unwilling to be accused of perjury because he'd lied under oath.

And the truth was that Dr. Wilson Turner had been in no condition to operate that morning. Just as he had been in no condition to operate several times before. The only difference was that this time, his luck had run out. As had Miguel Ortiz's.

Jenny paused to let this crucial bit of information sink in before she addressed the jury.

"My worthy opponent maintains that Dr. Kennedy and Nurse Jacobs exaggerated the situation. That Dr. Turner was nowhere near as badly off as they claim." Pivoting on her heel, Jenny swung around in Miguel's direction, gesturing toward him. "Yet Mr. Ortiz cannot walk, cannot face a day without pain.

"My worthy opponent tells you that no one is perfect. That we all slip once in a while and that no malice was intended. All of this is true. Dr. Turner did not intentionally botch the surgery. No, what he did was try to anesthetize himself against his own pain."

She looked at the doctor sitting at the opposing table flanked by two of the hospital's lawyers. He looked on the brink of a breakdown. It pained her to continue, but she wasn't here to help soothe his conscience; she was here to do right by her client.

"His wife had left him earlier that week. Because of his drinking," she emphasized. "So he drank to dull the pain. Then went to Mercy General to operate on Miguel Ortiz." Her voice was low, but powerful as she attacked the heart of the matter. "Would you have wanted him operating on you?

"The first line of the Hippocratic oath—'First do no harm'—should have compelled Dr. Turner to excuse himself from picking up a scalpel. But Dr. Turner did a great deal of harm. And because of what he did, Mr. Ortiz will never again be able to dance with his wife or live one day without pain, pain that serves as a constant reminder of what Wilson Turner did to him.

"If that is not the clearest definition of 'pain and suffering,' ladies and gentlemen, then I don't know what is. I want you to remember that as you go into that chamber. When you emerge again, I hope you will award Mr. Ortiz the maximum amount permitted under the law."

Having concluded, Jenny retreated to her side of the courtroom. She listened as the judge instructed the jury, his voice a dull buzz in her ears, her heart hammering wildly in her chest. She'd done all she could.

She turned and looked toward the back of the courtroom, filled with friends and former coworkers of Miguel's, as well as some supporters.

She saw none of them. She was looking for Eric. When she noticed the seat he'd occupied earlier was vacant, a kernel of disappointment popped inside of her, but she squelched it. If she'd been hoping that he'd see her at her best, she dismissed it as a foolish thought, something worthy of an adolescent in a high school play.

But this wasn't a performance, this was reality. And she wasn't Cinderella, hoping to be noticed by her prince.

With all her heart, she wished Jordan hadn't meddled, hadn't taken it upon himself to ask Eric to take part in the auction.

Turning back around, she saw the jury filing out to be sequestered. Jenny crossed her fingers.

Jenny got out of the taxi and paid the driver. All in all, considering its less than spectacular start, it hadn't been that bad a day.

There was no word back from the jury yet. She knew it was going to take time, but she had every reason to hope that it would be a good word once they received it. Mercy General's battalion of lawyers had looked less than pleased by the time the jury had been led away.

And, she reminded herself as she unlocked her apartment door, she had landed Eric Logan for the bachelor auction.

Well, she hadn't, but Jordan had.

In either case, that really was a good thing, her own feelings notwithstanding.

"Terrific, so you get to auction him off to some oversexed socialite with polished nails and too much time on her hands."

She glanced down at her own nails as she put her keys away. The tips were small and round. If she let them grow, they insisted on breaking. No matter what her mother wished for, she just wasn't the idle, socialite type.

"How great is that going to feel?" she asked herself a bit too loudly.

"Excuse me?"

She had to stop doing that, Jenny thought. She had to stop talking out loud to herself and forgetting that there were other people around. She grinned at the woman at the kitchen sink.

"Sorry, Sandra, I was just talking to myself." She slipped off her coat. "So, how is everything?"

Drying her hands, Sandra looked over her shoulder at the boy who was sitting on the sofa, playing with a single beat-up action figure. One his mother had given him.

She crossed over to Jenny and lowered her voice. "'Everything' is fine. The teacher said he even played a little with the other children. Five minutes or so, but that is progress."

Five minutes or so wasn't very much in the scope of a six-hour day, especially not when Cole had always been a happy, lively child, but it was a start.

Jenny grinned. "Yes, it is. Baby steps, right Cole?"

She pushed her briefcase under the kitchen chair, out of the way. She swore to herself that tonight she wasn't going to look at anything, not even the new case she'd had to take on at the last minute after she'd headed back to the office.

Tonight was going to be about Cole.

And, she thought wearily, about pulling the strings together for the auction. She had to be sure to get Eric's and Peter's names on the list. There was no doubt that the Logan brothers would bring more women to the gala. More women, more money.

And, a small voice reminded her, while those women pushed the bidding higher and higher, she'd be on the sidelines watching. She dismissed the niggling thought. Watching was good, too. After all, someone had to do it.

Crossing to the living room sofa, she opened her arms to Cole. When the little boy made no attempt to get up or move to her, she bent down to him and gave him a hug. After a moment, he returned it. It was halfhearted, somewhat mechanical but it still gladdened her.

"Will there be anything else, Miss Jenny?"

Jenny shook her head, more to herself than in response to what the older woman asked her. Over the last six months she'd tried countless times to get Sandra to just call her Jenny and stop putting "Miss" in front of her name, but it seemed a lesson that the woman refused to learn.

The first time she'd made the request of the bright-eyed Filipino woman, Sandra had informed her that there had to be a set decorum between employer and employee. That, Sandra had added quietly, had been her mother's way and her grandmother's way before her and they had both had long, fulfilling careers as housekeepers for some of the best families in the country. Sandra ignored too Jenny's reminder that her duties involved only watching over and entertaining Cole, not housekeeping. Hence not only did Jenny manage to get a spotless child out of the bargain, but a spotless apartment, as well. The only way she finally assuaged her guilty conscience was to pay the older woman more than had been originally agreed upon.

All ninety-eight pounds of Sandra stood before her now, waiting for further instructions, even though they both knew it was time for her to go home to her own family. "No, Sandra, thank you."

Sandra nodded her dark head as she returned to the kitchen to take her purse out of the bottom cupboard where she kept it.

"Then I'll be going home now." She hoisted the strap onto a shoulder that looked thin and bony even beneath her winter coat. "I'll be here early tomorrow."

Jenny twisted around on the sofa to look at her. "Early? Why?"

Sandra's expression told Jenny she was clearly bewildered that she should ask. "Why, to make up for being late today, of course."

The woman was already the poster-child for the perfect household employee. "Sandra, there's no need to 'make up' for anything. You were a little late. You're human. It happens."

But Sandra shook her head. It was clearly not an issue to be discussed. "You are too understanding,

Miss Jenny. People will start to think that they can walk all over you."

Jenny smiled as she nestled back onto the sofa with Cole. "I'll have you to watch my back, Sandra. I'll be safe."

At the door, Sandra paused before opening it, her dark eyes sweeping over them. "You look natural that way, Miss Jenny." There was deep-rooted approval in her voice. "Just like mother and son."

Jenny kissed the top of Cole's head. The boy seemed not to notice.

"Thanks," she whispered. "See you tomorrow."

"Early," Sandra insisted, then closed the door behind her.

Jenny laughed softly to herself. The slight shaking of her chest had Cole looking up at her. "Oh, so you finally noticed something, did you? How about this? Did you notice this?"

Lifting the hem of his white and red striped shirt, Jenny pressed her lips against Cole's small, rounded tummy and blew just hard enough against his skin to tickle him. It was something she used to do with him, something that was guaranteed to reduce him into a fit of giggles. He scrunched up now, as if trying to squirm away, but he did laugh and the sound made her heart feel as if it was overflowing.

Baby steps, she repeated to herself.

As long as those baby steps were going in the right direction, she could wait them out until they finally arrived at their destination.

Until Cole was himself again.

She tightened her arms around him protectively as she thought of her mother's visit last night. She knew her mother wasn't trying to be hurtful, that in her own strange, isolated way she was trying to do the best for her. But this *was* best for her, being Cole's mother. There was no way in the world that she was going to give Cole up, even if she hadn't promised Rachel that she would look after him.

She'd been there, as Rachel's coach, the day Cole was born. She saw him enter the world and she was the first to hold him. It was a case of love at first sight on her part.

A little like with her and Eric, she mused now, cradling Cole against her. But at least with Cole, there was hope for something more. With Eric, she knew that hope was just another four-letter word, one doomed not to flower. Attraction there was also one-sided. And there was never going to be another side to it. Ever. She knew that as far as he was concerned, she was just Jordan's sister, a shadow in the background. She remembered the first time she'd ever laid eyes on him. Jordan had brought him home for dinner. Eric had nodded and smiled at her when introductions were made. She doubted if he could have picked her out of a lineup two minutes later. All these years later, there'd been no progress.

"You're all the man I need, Cole," she said out loud, looking down at the boy in her lap. Maybe it was her imagination, but she could have sworn the boy curled into her a little more. Jenny smiled to herself and took heart.

Someday.

Five

Everett Baker stared at the newspaper section that was spread out before him on his overly neat desk in the accounting department at Children's Connection. He'd been looking through the various sections to distract himself from the fact that he was taking his lunch alone today. Again.

Friends were not something Everett ever had a gift for making. The people he could look to as something more than just passing acquaintances were few and far in between. He had never really gotten comfortable with being alone, either, but it was a fact of life that he had come to accept the way someone accepts a physical defect.

After all these years, he had come to learn how to live with loneliness. Sort of.

He stared at the caption on page two. Every time he tried to forget, to come to terms with his past, his life, fate found a way to remind him. Life had given him a rough deal.

A wistful sigh escaped his thin lips.

It hadn't always been that way. Once he'd been happy. Once, a very long time ago, so long ago that it felt as if it had happened to someone else or was a fairy tale he'd read so often that it had become real for him, he'd been loved and felt secure. Back then in that faraway yesterday, he'd had two parents who loved and doted on him; he'd lived in a beautiful house and had everything he wanted.

But that was before he'd been taken. Stolen off the peaceful streets of Spring Heights, right in front of his best friend Danny Crosby's house. And all because he'd tried to help.

He'd believed Lester Baker that first time he'd seen the man, believed him when Lester had told him that he was searching for his puppy and needed help. He'd been Robbie Logan back then and he'd paid for his kind heart a thousand times over.

Abducted, he was forced to live with his kidnapper and the man's nearly insane wife, Joleen—two people he was forced to regard as his parents. Eventually, he'd believed them when they'd told him that his own parents hadn't wanted him, had sold him to them. Hope ebbed away, leaving within him a void as huge as the Grand Canyon.

The three of them had traveled from place to place, always a jump ahead of the law, always living in squalor. There'd been so many places that eventually, he forgot where he belonged and to whom.

Until his "mother's" death-bed confession had both set him free and by the same stroke, further imprisoned him, giving him a life sentence. Trapping him in the life he hated while seductively whispering that once, things had been different. Would still be different. If only…

If only…

He'd discovered that his real name was Robert—Robbie—Logan and that his real parents were Terrence and Leslie Logan, the kind, loving parents who used to come to him in dreams. As soon as he knew the truth, he'd wanted to go to them, to declare that he was the son they'd lost and looked for for so many years. But life with Joleen and Lester Baker had broken his spirit, sapped it from him and turned him into a man who thought too much and saw sunsets where sunrises should be.

He felt that the Logans wouldn't want him the way he was now. Why should they?

In the years since he'd been Robbie Logan, his parents had gone on to have more sons, more children, both natural and adopted. They'd become richer and more well known, in the worlds of industry and charity alike. They were the ones who largely funded the Children's Connection, an organization that helped loving couples connect with children who needed love and to adopt them. He'd learned that reading an article on the organization and had immediately sought out a job there.

It was as close as he'd allow himself to get to the family he never stopped longing for in his heart.

They wouldn't want him now. He really wasn't a Logan anymore. Wasn't a Baker. Wasn't anything except a man on the outside, wistfully looking in. A man who didn't want to deal with the final, ultimate rejection of having his family turn away from him.

So he never outed himself in that position. He remained hidden.

What had caused him to stop eating the meager ham sandwich he'd made for himself this morning was the story he discovered in the human interest section. The Parent Adoption Network, which was closely associated with both Portland General Hospital and Children's Connection, was holding its annual bachelor auction. Two of his brothers—the brothers who were completely unaware of his existence—were listed among the eligible men who were participating in the auction.

Despair filled him. Not that he was missing out on a social gala, he could care less about that. The spear to his heart was that he would never see his name listed alongside of his brothers in this manner.

He'd never be anything but what he was. A man doomed to face life alone.

Very carefully Everett folded the sides of the wax paper back around his half eaten sandwich. And then he crumpled it before throwing it into the wastepaper basket.

He'd lost his appetite.

You'd think that she was one of the women who were sitting in the audience, waiting for the auction to begin. Waiting to bid on a desirable man.

Probably if she was, the size of the butterflies that were launching themselves like kamikaze pilots in her stomach would have been smaller.

Jenny pressed her hand against her stomach, trying to will it into stillness. She was just conducting an auction, nothing more. Why couldn't she remember that?

Although she never felt her best in social situations, she hadn't felt like this last year.

Last year, she reminded herself, Eric Logan hadn't been one of the participants.

That wasn't supposed to make a difference.

It did.

She pressed harder against her stomach, praying that her lunch wasn't going to come back up and make a reappearance.

"Wow, you look pale." Coming up behind her, Jordan circled the podium until he was facing his sister. "Even for you," he qualified. His eyes swept over her face. "You okay?"

"Peachy." She turned from the podium and the

various index cards she had piled there that gave pertinent, vital information about the men she was going to be auctioning off. She'd made notations on the ones she'd gotten earlier, trying to say something light about each participant. She still didn't have Eric's.

And here's the man I've been in love with since I graduated from a training bra, ladies. Try not to mangle him.

She smiled at her brother. "Thanks again for getting Eric and Peter to join in. Tickets to this event absolutely went through the roof." She nodded toward the ballroom that was filling up prodigiously. "There isn't a chair left. They're really going to be packed in here."

Looking out on the growing crowd, Jordan pretended to take offense. "How do you know they're not all flocking here to see me?"

Jenny looked at her older brother, trying to see him through impartial eyes. He had grown up to be a very darkly handsome man. Not as startling handsome as Eric—few achieved that kind of perfect, she thought—but very good-looking in his own right.

And right now, he was angling for a compliment. Being his sister, she couldn't be the one giving it to him.

Instead, she smiled prettily at him and murmured, "Intuition, dear brother, intuition."

"Here." Leaning over, he placed his 4-by-5 index card on top of the rest, then tugged his cuffs into place as he straightened again. "Feel free to add in any flattering adjectives you feel might up the bidding."

She picked up the card and scanned it quickly. She grinned at the description he'd crafted and raised her eyes to meet his. "How does 'cute but dictatorial' sound?"

His eyes held hers. "Like you're describing yourself."

The frown sprang to her lips instantly. She didn't mind being teased, but she resented being laughed at. Even by her own brother. "I'm not cute, Jordan, and we both know it."

He moved behind her. "Only one of us knows the truth about that."

She squealed as he pulled out three hairpins. Her hand flew to her hair, but the damage was already done. There were loose strands everywhere. "What do you think you're doing?"

He pushed away her hands and fanned out her hair. "Ushering you out of the nineteenth century. Men like hair on women, Jenny. Long, flowing hair." He threw out a few more pins.

"What difference does it make what they like?" There was a defensive edge to her voice. "I'm the one auctioning them off, not taking them home with me."

He stood back, as if to admire his handiwork. "Maybe if you're good, they'll let you have the leftovers."

"If I'm good," she countered, "there aren't going to be any leftovers."

The light, seductive scent of cologne flirted with her senses, drifting in from behind her. She stiffened. Eric. She wasn't aware of swallowing before turning in his direction.

Just in time to brush up against one very hard chest. Every single nerve in her body knotted, threatening to choke her.

Stepping back to avoid a collision, Eric held out the index card in his hand. "Is this where I sign up to be humiliated?"

Because her brother was there, watching, Jenny recovered faster than she might have. Embarrassment did not welcome witnesses, even related ones.

"Why humiliated?" she asked, doing her very best to sound blasé, or at least anything short of what she was, which was flustered.

"Well, for one thing," Eric pointed out, "what if no one bids?"

She laughed, shaking her head. He couldn't possibly be that modest. Or that unaware of himself. Mirrors vied for the man's reflection.

"That's like saying what if the sun doesn't set tonight. It's a sure thing." She glanced toward her brother, drawing him into her observation. "You are part of the beautiful men. You're what women dream about at night. We're allowing them, for a sizable donation, to see what it feels like to have their dream come true for an evening." It was the premise behind the auction. That and gathering sizable contributions for the foundation.

Eric dismissed the compliment. "I see your honeyed tongue isn't restricted to the courtroom."

Jordan raised an eyebrow. "You saw Jenny in court?" He looked from one to the other, as if waiting for one of them to respond.

Jenny ignored him, her attention focused instead on Eric's comment. There was no way he could accurately make that statement about her talent in court. "You left the courtroom before I got to the summation."

"I heard enough to convince me that if I ever need a lawyer, I'm coming to you."

No, you're not going to blush. You're a grown woman, and women over the age of twelve don't blush. She clenched her hands into fists, willing the color to stay down. It felt like a losing battle.

Eric stood back, cocking his head as he studied her. It made her shift uneasily. "You've done something different with your hair."

Her hair. Oh, God, she probably looked like a wild woman. Horrified, her hand flew to her wayward tresses, but there was no way she could pin them back without a mirror and a brush.

She shot an accusing look at Jordan. "That's Jordan's fault. He suddenly decided that he wanted to play hairdresser."

The information made Eric grin at his best friend. "I didn't know you had hidden talents, Jordan." His eyes shifted back to Jenny. "I'd say you might have a real future ahead of you."

In turn Jordan grinned at Jenny, as if to say, "See? I told you so."

She groaned. "Don't encourage him, Eric. His head's big enough as it is." In self-defense, she looked at the card that Eric had placed beside her brother's. There was little on it. "You just wrote down your name, height and age."

Eric shrugged, his broad shoulders moving ever so slightly within the custom-made jacket. "I didn't bother putting down where I worked. I figured you already knew that."

Everyone already knew that, she thought. "This isn't a driver's license application, Eric. You're supposed to put down your likes, dislikes, things like that." She was more than a little interested in that herself. She held the card out to him. "I need a little something more to work with."

He pushed the card back into her fingers. "From what I've seen, you do well on your feet, Jen. If it needs jazzing up, I trust you to do it."

And then his warm smile faded as he looked over her head and saw someone in the crowd at the other end of the ballroom.

It was like watching the sun suddenly go out, she thought. Jenny turned and looked in the general direction she assumed Eric was looking in. Had he seen an old flame? Someone he was trying to avoid?

"Is something wrong, Eric?" she heard herself asking him.

"No, nothing." But it was clear by his tone that something was.

She scanned the room, and her eyes lit on a potential reason for Eric's sudden change in deportment. There, talking to several people, was Trent Crosby. Jenny suddenly recalled the bad blood between the Crosbys and the Logans.

The Crosbys were the reason that Robbie Logan, the brother Eric had never met, had been kidnapped and killed. Trent's mother, Sheila, was supposed to have been watching Robbie and her own son, Danny, at play. Instead, she'd been on the phone. Rumor had it that she'd been talking to her lover of the moment, begging him not to leave her.

True or not, it had kept her from watching the boys, kept her from saving Robbie when he needed her. Consequently, Robbie had been kidnapped and never recovered. Terrence and Leslie Logan never forgave Sheila.

Eric picked up a program and scanned the names of the men participating in the auction. "Did you ask Trent Crosby to be part of this?"

She'd completely forgotten how he might react to that. But she'd had to invite Trent. The Crosbys were generous contributors to charities in their own right and she couldn't afford to insult them by deliberately omitting a representative from their family.

Jenny looked to Jordan for help. He raised his shoulders in a helpless shrug. Desperation had her saying, “Why don’t the two of you grab a drink at the bar, unwind a little before the big moment?”

“Sounds good to me.” Jordan moved in front of Eric, as if ready to lead the way to the bar that ran along the side wall.

Eric shrugged. “Sure, why not.” He looked at Jenny, flashing her a grin that was not as easy as it might have been. “See you later, gorgeous.”

She tried not to let the word seduce her. He probably said that to all the females he met and meant nothing by it. Jenny blew out a long breath. With effort, she forced her mind back on the auction.

One crisis averted, five million to go.

Six

"Do you have any idea who that woman is with Trent Crosby?"

Jordan and Eric both ordered a Scotch on the rocks, the same drink that Peter had been nursing when they joined him at the bar. They'd no sooner gotten their drinks than Peter nodded toward the far end of the room and asked his question.

Eric turned in the general direction his brother was looking. The woman had sun-streaked brown hair and was wearing an emerald-green evening gown that revealed a killer figure.

Taking a sip of his drink, he shook his head. "Haven't a clue." He made the most logical guess. "Probably a girlfriend of his." And then he peered closer at his brother. "Why? You interested?" Even as he asked, a grin took over his features. When was Peter not interested in a beautiful woman?

"Definitely," Peter murmured, still looking at the woman. It was a known fact that when he worked, he worked hard. The same could be said for when he played. Peter didn't believe in doing things by half measures.

Eric turned and looked at his older brother. "I have to confess I'm still a little surprised to actually see you here for this event. I didn't think your 'dance card' was free for the next six months."

"The CEO showing up at a charity event is a good thing for the Logan Corporation," Peter told him glibly. "Especially since Mom and Dad are so closely associated with PAN." And then he looked back toward the woman beside Trent Crosby. "Think she'll be bidding?"

"Hey, bidding or not, why don't you make a move?" Eric took another sip of his drink. He couldn't remember the last time he had to say something to motivate his older brother when it came to anything, least of all a woman. "Nothing in the rules about not making any 'independent contacts' while we're all here, baring our souls for the good of charity." He looked to Jordan for confirmation.

The latter nodded as if on cue.

With a laugh, Eric took hold of Peter's shoulder and pointed him in the general direction of the young woman. "Go for it, big brother. While you're at it, see if she's got a friend for me." He winked broadly.

There was still one huge hurdle none of them had mentioned. "But she's with Trent Crosby." And there was bad blood there.

Eric shrugged. "Way I see it, all the more reason to win her away. What you need is a distraction." He glanced back toward Jenny, an idea forming. "And I'm going to provide it for you." His grin broadened as he looked at Peter. He liked the idea of being his older brother's sidekick. They didn't socialize together as much as he would have enjoyed. "Wait here, and as soon as the young lady's alone, make your move." He looked at Jordan. "You watch his back."

"The invasion at Normandy took less coordination," Jordan murmured, but it was clear that he was getting a kick out of this, as well. Eric was already on his mission.

Eric startled her. She'd just been watching Maggie Sullivan, a social worker whose ties, professional as well as emotional, were with the foundation, talking to one of the bachelors. The woman looked as nervous as she felt. Eric coming up behind her didn't help matters any. She'd almost yelped.

She didn't like people coming up behind her. Since she already felt herself lacking, whenever she was in a social gathering, she liked being prepared for all contingencies, not being caught off guard.

Eric always caught her off guard.

"Do me a favor, Jen."

His breath zipped along her bare back, creating havoc on her entire nervous system.

Anything. Bear your children, walk barefoot in the snow. You name it, I'm your woman.

God, but I like the sound of that.

Exercising mind over matter, Jenny managed to keep her expression from betraying her thoughts as she turned around to face him. "What is it?"

Eric nodded back toward the couple at the far end of the room. "Call Trent Crosby over here."

She wanted to understand. "Why?"

The grin he gave her almost melted her lacy underwear. "Because I'm playing Cupid."

She blinked, drawing her mind back into the world of the functioning. "Excuse me?"

"Peter wants to meet the woman with Crosby and, the only way he can probably get near her is if Crosby's occupied. I'm asking you to occupy Trent Crosby for a few minutes. For Peter's sake." He leaned in to her, as if confiding some huge secret. He winked at her broadly and grinned. "He doesn't get out much."

Right, and she was secretly a Hollywood movie star. She looked over and saw that Trent was talking to Katie. A remarkably made-over Katie, but it was still Katie Crosby. Trent's sister. And Peter wanted to talk to her? It didn't add up.

She looked back toward Eric. The man was standing much too close to her. Not reacting or allowing her mind to drift was a tremendous challenge.

"Do you know who that woman is?" Jenny asked. "That's—"

"The first woman Peter has expressed any real interest in since the Ice Age," Eric told her, cutting in. "C'mon, Jen, be a pal."

She wanted to be a great deal more than that, but pal was good, she told herself. At least it was better than a stranger. And it was a start.

Taking a breath, she nodded. "Sure."

Eric brushed a kiss against her cheek. "Thanks."

"Don't mention it," she murmured, trying vainly to gather together her suddenly scattered senses from the four corners of the room.

It took her a second to coax her heart out of her throat so that she could speak rather than squeak.

Leaning over the microphone at the podium, gripping the sides for support, she asked, "Will Mr. Trent Crosby approach the podium, please? Trent Crosby," she repeated, hoping that by the time the man approached, she could actually think again.

Stepping away, Eric turned and gave her the high sign just before melting into the crowd.

Trent came striding up to the podium a couple of minutes later. "Hi. Jennifer, right?" He didn't wait for her to nod, or contradict him. "You wanted to see me about something?"

Without Eric at her elbow, she could think again. Jenny smiled brightly at the man before her. "Yes, I wanted to give you your number in the auction." She handed him a button that denoted his position on the program. "Just put it on your breast pocket," she advised. "And I also need your card."

"Oh, right."

As Trent dug into his pocket to find the card, Jenny looked over his shoulder to see that Peter Logan was approaching Katie Crosby. Maybe the rift between the two families was finally going to be mended, she thought. And that was a good thing. Life was too short to spend it at odds with people.

Life's too short to spend like a cloistered nun. That had been her mother's pronouncement, delivered while staring pointedly at her. But that, Jenny thought, was a whole different matter.

Turning away, she saw Eric being approached by a tall, good-looking woman dressed in a shimmering black sequined gown. Nothing subtle about Melody Maguire, she thought. That probably went for the play she was guessing the woman was making for Eric.

Business, Jenny. Get your mind back on business, she admonished herself.

Even so, she could still feel her cheek throbbing where Eric's lips had touched it.

"I can't tell you how grateful I am that you decided to take part in our little auction this year," Melody was gushing.

As a good-looking male, Eric was accustomed to

being looked at a certain way. Usually, he found it flattering. This time, he wasn't quite sure. "Don't thank me, thank Jenny Hall. She's the one who signed me up."

The woman's smile was just this side of condescending. She waved a hand in the general direction of the podium, her dark eyes all but devouring him like hungry little piranha.

"Yes, that's our little Jenny. A great little go-getter. Too bad she's all work, no play. I've always valued play myself," Melody breathed, running her hand slowly along his arm. She looked up at him with wide, not-so-innocent eyes. "It's so good for the soul, don't you think?"

"Absolutely." Eric looked around, wondering where Jordan went to. The woman, although very attractive, was a man-eater of the first degree, and he was in definite need of rescuing.

Melody cocked her head, her bottle-assisted red hair tumbling provocatively onto her bare shoulder. "So tell me, what do you think your best attributes are?"

Not being rude to overbearing women. Eric nodded toward the podium. "I already wrote a few things down for Jenny," he lied.

"Oh, that." Melody waved a dismissive, bejeweled hand. A ten-carat diamond on her finger flashed like trapped lightning, a gift from her last, late husband. "I never pay attention to secondhand information. I like getting mine straight from the horse's mouth." She smiled at him much like he thought a snake might—if a snake could smile—just before it struck. "So to speak," she concluded.

Watching them from across the room, Jenny tried to ignore her sinking feeling. She knew one woman who was going to be bidding for Eric, she thought. The woman was a barracuda, but Eric didn't seem to mind. Maybe he liked them bold and brassy.

That certainly left her out of the race.

As if she could ever get in it.

Annoyed with herself, Jenny forced her mind back on the auction. She glanced at her watch.

It was almost time.

Jenny paused to take a sip from the glass resting on the shelf inside the podium. Her throat felt parched. She'd been at this for over an hour.

The evening was going far better than she or the people on the Parent Adoption Network board who had planned this evening's event could have hoped for. Fifteen of the twenty men had been auctioned off to the highest bidder, and every single one of the eligible bachelors had brought in a great deal of money.

It helped, she thought, to assuage the pang she was feeling about having to auction off Eric. She banged down the gavel again, "selling" Alan Couffee for an evening of fun at the Portland Performing Arts Theater, followed by dinner at the exclusive Chandler Club, to Juliana Richter for fifteen hundred dollars.

As she picked up the next card, she saw that her brother was finally up on the auction block.

Standing in the wings beside Jordan, Eric watched the smile blossom on Jenny's lips. "You know, you're sister's prettier than she thinks she is."

"Trying for a degree in psychology?" Jordan teased, straightening his tie.

"No, but you can tell by the way she carries herself that she doesn't think she's very attractive. She is. You should say something to her."

Jordan laughed shortly. "Would either of your sisters listen to anything you said?"

"You have a point."

"Shh." Jordan held up his hand, silencing his friend. "I'm up."

"And now, ladies," Jenny was saying, "I give you my brother, Jordan Hall." She paused, waiting for Jordan to make his entrance. He did cut a good figure, she thought dispassionately. Too bad the family looks ran out after he was born. "Believe me," she said, leaning over the microphone, "there were years in which I would have done exactly that—given you my brother—and sweetened the pot by throwing in my home entertainment center, as well.

"But now a successful lawyer with Morisson and Treherne, my brother has done very well for himself. A date with Jordan will bring you a racing pulse and a day at the exclusive Steeple Hills Horse Ranch, so this one's for you athletic ladies. And the one thing

I can honestly tell you is that Jordan knows how to treat a lady."

She let that sink in, watching the way many of the women were reacting to her brother. Family pride filled her. "Shall we start the bidding at—"

"A thousand dollars," a woman in the back of the ballroom declared, waving her program.

And they're off, Jenny thought.

Bidding went quite rapidly, topping off at almost five thousand dollars before it was finally over. After repeating the figure three times, Jenny banged down her gavel, ending the round.

She glanced toward her brother. "Boy, if I'd known you were going to go for that high a price, I would have tried selling you a long time ago."

Jordan looked over his shoulder at her. "Brat," he mouthed affectionately as he left the stage.

She didn't have to look down at the next card. She knew it belonged to Eric.

This should be easy, she thought. On everyone but her.

Still, she knew this was going to happen when she signed him up for it. She could see Melody positioning herself to rush into the bidding. Several other women moved to the edge of their seats, as if poised to jump in, as well.

There'd be no shortage of money here, she thought. Who knew, maybe if she were sitting on the other side of the podium, she might have been tempted to bid herself.

Who was she kidding? As if she'd ever have the nerve, she mocked herself.

Time to get on with it. She cleared her throat, then waved Eric forward.

"And now we have a gentleman who needs no introduction. Eric Logan—"

"Two thousand," Melody declared, catching everyone else off guard, including Jenny.

She'd been about to read the notes she'd jotted down herself on Eric's card, but since Melody had opened up the bidding, there was no need to recite the statistics. Forcing a smile to her lips, Jenny set the card facedown on the large "finished" pile.

She looked across the room at Melody. "I guess you don't need to hear about the kind of evening Eric has planned—"

"Two thousand one hundred."

Jenny looked to her left to see that Lola Wilcox, a woman she'd thought of as a friend, had raised her hand and thrown her hat into the proceedings. Tall, blond, willowy, Lola was just as vivacious as Melody, but more subtle. Of the two Lola undoubtedly offered Eric the more enjoyable evening. Jenny knew she should be thinking of Eric's comfort, but there were other emotions at play here.

She looked out at the crowd. "Anyone else?"

Several other bids were offered, going up by small increments.

And then Melody jumped into the arena again. "Two thousand five hundred."

"Two thousand five hundred fifty."

Another county heard from, Jenny thought as she took in the latest bid.

The next moment Lola trumped the bid, only to be topped by Melody.

The bidding was heated for a few minutes as several women tried besting one another. But as the bidding escalated higher, one by one, the other women were forced to drop out, leaving only Melody and Lola bidding against each other.

Every time Melody upped her bid, Lola would add fifty dollars to it.

When the bidding hit seven thousand, Jenny was absolutely astonished. "Ladies, I want you to remember this is just for an evening. You're not buying the man outright." Eric was to her left and she heard him chuckling. The sound warmed her but she didn't dare look in his direction.

"Seven thousand five hundred," Melody announced.

Jenny looked toward Lola, who'd suddenly grown quiet. It looked as if Melody was going to walk off with an evening with Eric after all.

"Seven thousand five hundred going once." Gavel poised, Jenny scanned the audience. A hush had fallen over the women. "Going twice." She raised her gavel higher, ready to bring it down and conclude the bidding, when Lola seemed suddenly to come to life.

"Ten thousand dollars."

The gavel almost slipped from Jenny's fingers.

This amount was far and away more money than they had ever gotten before.

"You do realize you have to give him back," she said to Lola. The woman nodded. Jenny's eyes shifted toward Melody.

But the latter shook her head. "Too rich for my blood," Melody said. She winked at Eric. "Catch you later, sugar."

Jenny blew out a breath. Ten thousand dollars. A woman spending that kind of money had a right to expect a lot, charity or no charity. She refused to let her mind go there.

Forcing a smile to her lips, she raised her gavel again. "All right, ten thousand dollars going once, going twice—" Jenny paused for a beat, then brought down the gavel. "Sold to Lola Wilcox for ten thousand dollars. PAN thanks you," she heard herself saying automatically. Lola returned her smile and nodded.

Jenny was vaguely aware of Eric fading back behind the curtain again. She hardly remembered getting through the rest of the auction. There were three more eligible bachelors to clear from the boards before the event was finally over.

As each of the evening's winners came up, one by one, to claim their certificates for their dates, Jenny tried to keep her mind on her work and not on how strangely empty she felt.

Probably because this was the last contact she'd have with Eric, she told herself.

She supposed there was always next year's auction. If he wasn't married to Lola by then, she qualified sarcastically.

Lola was the last in line.

Fitting, Jenny thought.

"You certainly got carried away there," Jenny commented.

"It was for a good cause," Lola responded. She held out the check to her. Rather than a partial payment, it was made out for the full amount. Jenny expected nothing less.

"That it was." Taking the check, she placed it with the others inside a large manila envelope and marked "paid in full" next to Lola's name on the list. "I know you'll make the most of this."

She handed Lola the certificate. Across the top she'd written in Eric's name. In flowery letters, the certificate said it entitled the bearer to one date, lasting no less than three hours, no more than twenty-four, to the above listed bachelor.

"Yes, I will," Lola assured her.

She handed the certificate back to Jenny.

Jenny stared at the paper. Was there something wrong with the wording?

"What are you doing?" she asked.

"Handing the certificate to the woman who's going to be Eric Logan's date."

Seven

When Jenny made no move to take the certificate, Lola physically opened her hand and placed the paper in it.

Jenny raised her eyes to Lola's face. "Is this your idea of a joke?"

"No, this is my idea of being deadly serious." She pushed Jenny's hand away. "Much as the idea is tempting, Jenny, I can't go out with Eric, at least not under these circumstances."

None of this was making any sense to her. Jenny had a feeling she was waiting for some punch line that was too slow in coming.

"What circumstances? You won the auction fair and square, although I did think you went a little overboard in the bidding." No evening with a man was worth that price tag, unless you had so much money to burn that it was positively sinful.

Lola shrugged, then tugged at the top of her bodice to keep the evening gown from slipping down too far and bringing new meaning to the term plunging neckline. "I wasn't using my money."

Now this *really* wasn't making any sense. Jenny stared at the woman. "What are you talking about? Whose money were you using?"

Lola slipped her arm around Jenny's shoulders and pulled her close. Then she leaned in and whispered, "I'm a shill, Jenny. I represent a bunch of people who wanted to find a way to thank you for all the hard work you've put into this auction and all the other auctions and charitable functions you've presided over. They figured that giving you a big night out on the town was one way to show their appreciation." Lola smiled down at her. "You've got a big heart, Jenny. It's time someone said thank you. This is the best way we knew how." She ran the tip of her index finger over the top of the certificate. "Consider this Cinderella's invitation to the ball."

Her.

Eric.

Together.

On a date.

Like corks bobbing up and down in the water, the words just weren't sinking in.

"You're kidding," Jenny whispered.

Lola grinned. "No, I'm not."

This couldn't be real. She was dreaming. Or better yet, hallucinating. "You're kidding."

"No," Lola said a bit more firmly, "I'm not."

Jenny shook her head, utterly stunned. What was the catch? There had to be a catch. Things like this just didn't happen to her. "You're kidding."

Removing her arm from about Jenny's shoulders, Lola blew out a breath. "No, I'm not." And then she raised her hand before a fourth round of repetition could get underway. "I think we've already established that point." She peered at Jenny's face. "Look, would you like to sit down? You look a little pale."

Pale should have been the worst of her reaction. Pale was a color, or the absence of same. Right now, she was beyond the pale and smack in the middle of panic mode. What would she wear, what would she say? What would he say when he found out about the switch? He thought he was getting Lola, not her.

This was insane. She couldn't let this go any further. "I can't accept this."

Lola looked at her as if she actually saw the loose screws in her head. "Too late. It's yours."

"Then I give it to you." Jenny tried to push the certificate back into Lola's finely manicured hand.

Lola held both hands up, out of reach. "Sorry, I touch that certificate again and I'll turn into a pillar of salt, or go straight to the depths of hell or something equally as biblically frightening." And then her face softened in a genuine smile. "Relax, Jenny. Enjoy it. The gift comes from the heart. Accept it that way. Besides, aren't you and Eric Logan old friends?"

"We're not old anything," Jenny said, the words dribbling from her lips as she stared at the parchment in her hand.

Eric.

And her.

She couldn't even put them in the same sentence together, how was she going to place them in the same evening? She knew the answer to that. She couldn't.

Could she?

A giddiness began to form at the bottom of her toes, rising up through her like champagne in a bottle that had been suddenly shaken. Hard. The idea began to take hold. "This is insane, you know."

The smile on Lola's lips was one of growing satisfaction. "The best things usually are."

But there was a very real stumbling block to thwart the fairy tale in the making. "But what about Eric? He's going to be expecting to take you out."

"One step ahead of you," Lola told her proudly. "He's already been informed."

So Eric knew. Knew he wasn't going out with sleek, sophisticated Lola Wilcox and was, instead, going out with plain, sensible her. Jenny could just imagine how that conversation had gone. There was only one conclusion to be reached.

"Informed of what," she wanted to know, "that he's obligated to do a pity date?"

Lola looked at her as if she'd lost her mind, or at the very least, had temporary misplaced it. "No, that I was bidding for someone who was unable to. And since you were busy running the auction, you certainly weren't able to place any bids, were you?"

In her eyes, this was going from bad to worse. "So, instead of a pity date, he's going to think that I've been lusting after him all evening."

Lola obviously saw no shame in that. "Hey, why not? A lot of us were." She closed her eyes for a moment, a smile spreading out slowly, sensuously on her lips.

Watching her, Jenny had the distinct impression that Lola was visualizing Eric in various stages of undress. Especially when Lola opened her eyes again and there was a glow in them.

"That is one fine-looking man," Lola told her, "head to toe."

Lola made it sound as if she had firsthand insight into her pronouncement. Jenny couldn't help the question that came to her lips. "And you would know this how?"

Lola sighed wistfully. "I'd like to say personal contact, but I saw him jogging along the beach last summer. Bare-chested." She savored the word for a moment, then looked at Jenny. "My advice?"

Jenny was completely open to any and all suggestions. "Yes?"

"If, during the evening, he wants to get to third base, or home..." She paused significantly, then said, "Let him."

Right. As if that would ever even remotely cross his mind, Jenny thought. She closed her eyes. She still doubted that the man would even use his ticket to enter the ballpark, much less want to take part in the game.

"I'll keep that in mind." She straightened her shoulders slightly. "Tell whoever you were fronting for thank you."

Lola leaned over and brushed her lips against Jenny's cheek, barely making contact. "Enjoy."

Jenny heard a sincerity in the order. She nodded, her pulse suddenly launching into a tap dance. She looked down at the certificate again, half expecting it to have gone up in smoke.

She was still looking at it as Lola walked away.

The ballroom was thinning out. Jordan had already spoken to the woman who had won the bidding for an evening with him. Thalia Wellington promised to be an interesting, entertaining handful and he was looking forward to the date, arranged for a week from Friday because of their busy schedules.

But right now his mind was on his sister. He made eye contact with Lola and nodded. Satisfied with herself, the latter walked out of the ballroom.

Well, he reasoned, he'd done what he could. For the time being, anyway. The next step was up to Jenny.

A smile curved his mouth as he walked away. Funny how no matter how well you think you know yourself, there are always surprises out there. Never in a million years would he have thought of himself as a fairy godmother, yet that was exactly what he'd opted to be.

But it was for a good cause and he had to admit, it felt good, even if his bank account was ten thousand dollars lighter.

"So I hear you're my date."

Coming from behind, the deep masculine voice seemed to surround her, knocking her heart into double time.

Be cool, be cool. The advice didn't take, sliding down the icy slope of her fear.

Digging up a smile she could only hope wasn't sickly, Jenny turned around to face Eric.

The man was just too beautiful for words.

From somewhere, she managed to find her voice. "Um, about that—"

He cocked his head slightly. Endearingly. As if he was trying to gauge her mood and intent. "You're not backing out on me, are you?"

Right, like that would have ever happened to him. Women would walk on hot coals just to be close to Eric. Jenny knew she would. What she wouldn't do, though, was take advantage of a situation. Even though it was to her advantage.

"It's not a matter of backing out," she began, "I just don't think it's fair."

His eyes narrowed just a tad, as if he were trying to digest what she was saying. "I don't understand. Didn't you know about this?"

"No. Oh, God, no." She had to make him understand that she hadn't put anyone up to this. It was just too embarrassing otherwise.

He looked to see if he could find Lola, but the woman had already left. "But I was told that Lola did the bidding because you were obviously occupied at the moment and—"

"It's a trick," she cut in quickly. The words came out in a rush. "Some of my friends got together and thought this might be a way to repay me for the time I've volunteered to this cause—"

Was she making sense? Was she even speaking English, or was this all coming out as some kind of gibberish? She wasn't sure of anything, except that his eyes were beautiful and she was sinking into them as he stared at her.

He tried to understand what she was trying to tell him. "Then you don't want to go out with me?"

Her eyes widened. How could he even think that? Did he even *own* a mirror? "No!"

He interpreted her answer the only way he could. Eric stepped back. "Well then, I guess I should leave you alone."

Horrified, she was quick to rectify the mistake. "No, no, I mean, no." When he looked at her, confused, she knew she'd only made things worse. Jenny tried again. Where was her courtroom eloquence?

"That's not it. I do want to go out with you." It was still coming out wrong. She took a deep breath. "I mean, I didn't think this was fair to you."

He looked at her incredulously. "Me?"

"Yes." She got down to the heart of the matter. "You thought Lola was bidding on you."

He didn't follow. "What difference would that make? I didn't have any say in who was bidding on me. I knew that when I went into this thing. The understanding was that I would provide an evening of entertainment for whoever made the winning bid."

"And Lola made it—"

"For you," he pointed out. Maybe she was too polite to tell him that she didn't want to go out with him. Maybe there was someone else and wires had gotten crossed. "But if you don't want to go out with me, I can't exactly force you to."

Was he actually saying what she thought he was saying? What she *hoped* he was saying? "Then you're okay with this?"

He still didn't understand just what the problem was. "Sure, why wouldn't I be?"

Jenny pressed her lips together. This line of conversation had to end. She was sinking. Deeply and badly.

Reconnoitering, she decided that a fresh start was called for. Again, a giddiness began to infiltrate her system. She felt bubbly all over. "No reason," she replied to his question.

She was one of a kind, all right, Eric thought. "Okay then, when would be a good time for you?"

Now. Forever. Forcing her mind back to reality, Jenny mentally reviewed her schedule. She was going to be drowning in paperwork, preparing for the next court date. She had another case coming to court. And there was Mr. Ortiz. The jury was still playing Ping-Pong with the rest of his life. She had to be fresh and available for that. Which meant no late night out the night before. Jenny chewed on her lower lip, thinking.

Since she wasn't answering him, Eric made a stab at making arrangements himself. "How does this Friday night sound?"

"Um…"

He took the hesitation as a no. "Or Saturday. Would Saturday be better?"

"Saturday," she repeated, nodding her head because her tongue insisted on thickening and refused to work the way she needed it to.

Now that they had a day, he needed a time. "Seven? Eight?"

"Whatever." She knew herself, she'd be ready at dawn, counting off the seconds one by one until he came to her door. *If* he came to her door. Jenny still wasn't convinced that some part of her wasn't hallucinating all this. Had there been something in her water?

He nodded, as if making some kind of calculation. "Seven, then. Saturday at seven." His eyes swept over her and Jenny could have sworn that she felt them as they slowly went up and down her body.

Heat sprang up in response. She was surprised that she didn't spontaneously ignite. "Wear something fancy," he told her. "And if you don't mind—"

"Yes?" She was surprised she could push the word out across the arid terrain of her tongue. Deserts were probably less dry.

"Keep your hair down." He teased a curl away from her face. "I like it that way."

Thank you, Jordan. She owed him, she thought. A great deal.

"Hair. Down." Jenny repeated in staccato words. "Fine."

Eric laughed. It had been a long time since a woman he'd taken out had looked anything but amused and slightly jaded by the prospect. Jenny was like a breath of fresh air. He was going to enjoy this, he decided. Perhaps more than a little.

"Where do you live?"

The simple question bounced right off her head. "What?"

"Your address," he elaborated. "I'm going to need it." And then an amused expression highlighted his face, sending her pulse into overdrive. "Unless you'd like me to drive up and down the streets, shouting your name like Marlon Brando's character did in *A Streetcar Named Desire.*"

It took her a couple of seconds to actually remember it, but she finally rattled off her address for him.

Taking out his PalmPilot, something he rarely left

out of his sight, Eric entered the address, then slipped the silver object back into his jacket pocket. "So then it's a date. Next Saturday at seven."

"Date," she echoed, still feeling somewhat shell-shocked. This was all so surreal to her. This was her most cherished, most unrealistic daydream. And it was coming true.

Don't count your chickens yet....

Amused, unable to resist the bewitched expression on Jenny's face, Eric leaned over and lightly kissed her cheek again.

"See you then. And this was fun," he added. "I'm glad you asked me."

She didn't know if he was referring to the auction, or the date, but in either case he was wrong. Jordan was responsible for his being here and God only knew who all was responsible for his ultimately taking her out. And for creating the ulcer that was even now swiftly forming in her stomach.

But she didn't try to correct him. Talking with no saliva in your mouth was particularly difficult.

She was going to have to work on that, she told herself. Saturday was going to be here faster than she expected.

"Kidnapping?" Everett Baker repeated the loathsome word as if just having it on his tongue was painful for him.

At the sound of Baker's distress, the man on the other end of the line grew impatient. Patience had never been the Stork's long suit. Revenge was and he meant to exact it upon the Logans and everyone else he felt had been instrumental in keeping him down all these years. Those sickening do-gooders, the Logans, were just the tail end of a long list of people. People who would eventually be sorry they had gotten in his way.

They were in the business of selling black-market babies, although he'd had to drag an unwilling Baker into it. The miserable loner had a conscience, but he needed a man on the inside. So he'd befriended the man, slowly drawing him in until he was caught. Fortunately, along the way he'd stumbled across a piece of information he now used to blackmail Baker with. It kept him in line. And functioning.

The business was lucrative, even more so because there were only the three of them handling the details. Him, Baker and the man he had in place in Russia. Russia seemed as likely a place as any to "arrange" the so-called adoptions since it was happily out of the United States' jurisdiction. Barren women, desperate for babies to fill their arms if not their wombs, would drag their husbands to the ends of the earth to fulfill the maternal instincts that were chewing holes into their empty bellies.

Right now, a deal they had all thought was in place was showing all the signs of going sour on them. A young, unwed mother had promised them her baby when it was born. Then, without warning, she'd gone back on her word. She'd had a sudden qualm of conscience, wanting to mother the child she was bringing in the world.

All this sat very badly with the Stork, who had already promised the baby to someone. He didn't care what the hell the girl did or didn't do with her life, as long as it didn't interfere with his business.

But since it did, he had to make other plans. Money for her baby had already crossed hands. Money he wasn't about to give back. That meant he needed a baby.

Everett tried not to shudder. The mention of a kidnapping tied his stomach up in horrible, air-stealing knots. And brought with it a flood of memories that he was still desperately trying to eradicate from his brain.

He didn't want to be party to this. "I don't know about this. I don't think—"

"You're not being paid to think," the Stork snapped. "You're being paid to listen and to do as I say. That little bitch had no right to go back on the deal." He'd found out that arrangements had been made for the girl to give birth at Portland General. "You work at the Children's Connection, so it'll be a piece of cake. I want you to kidnap that little brat the second that bitch gives birth to it."

The thought of walking off with a baby filled Everett with fear. Despite the dank, cold weather, sweat began to pop out on his brow. "But how—"

"You're a clever guy, Baker, you'll come up with something."

The line went dead.

The darkness within Everett grew a little larger, a little lonelier.

Eight

Jenny sighed, taking a second to lean against the open closet. She peered into it, her eyes glazing over. The view didn't get any better.

She'd been a whirlwind of activity for the last hour, trying desperately to figure out what to wear when she went out with Eric. No fluttering fairy godmother had waved a magic wand to create just the perfect outfit hanging in the center of her ordinary clothing. No helpful mice, singing or otherwise, came to her aid, either.

Her closet was woefully unaccommodating.

She supposed she could always wear the same dress she'd worn to the auction, although the idea didn't really appeal to her. If nothing else, wearing the same dress her Prince Charming had already seen her in made her feel like a rerun.

That was what she got for being too busy to breathe.

All week, she'd meant to carve out an island of time for herself and go shopping for something new, something more fitting, to wear on her special evening. But the fates, it seemed, were determined that events would go otherwise. The jurors at Ortiz's trial had wanted some testimony reread to them and were still battling it out over the amount they felt they should recommend in the settlement.

She frowned. If that went on much longer, they ran the risk of being deadlocked. And then she and Miguel, not to mention his family, would have to go through the whole thing all over again. Just the thought was emotionally draining.

If that wasn't enough, she'd had three more cases added to her already burgeoning caseload. It had been difficult getting home at a decent hour, much less finding any time to shop.

Resigned, she reached into her closet and took out the mint green dress she'd worn to the auction.

Oh, well, nothing she wore was going to make the man fall head over heels in love with her.

Still, she had really wanted to come across as at least mildly attractive. She glanced in the mirror, her hand going to her hair. She'd already decided to leave it down, the way he favored, but that wasn't nearly enough to make her feel as pretty as she needed to feel in order to have a prayer of pulling off this date.

She had what it took to move through her parents' world—background, breeding. Everything except for confidence.

A new dress can't give you that, an annoying inner voice whispered. Maybe not, Jenny countered silently, but it certainly wouldn't have hurt.

"Miss Jenny?"

Holding the dress she'd resigned herself to, Jenny slid the mirrored door closed and turned to look at Sandra.

The woman's expression told her something was wrong. Her baby-sitter was not an alarmist by nature. Nor was she nearly as dramatic as Jenny's mother tended to be. "What is it?" she asked.

Sandra looked really torn, as if she didn't want to be the bearer of bad news but could see no other way around it.

"It's Cole, Miss Jenny. The boy has a fever. Do you want me to put him to bed and give him some Tylenol?"

Jenny's attention immediately shifted from dresses and other vapid considerations, directly to the precious life with which she'd been entrusted. Now that she thought about it, Cole had seemed more listless than usual today, but she'd attributed it to the weather.

"He's sick?" she asked as she hurried into the living room.

"It's just a small fever," Sandra responded.

Sandra had the little boy lying down on the sofa. He was curled up under his favorite blanket, a nearly threadbare cover he'd had ever since he was a baby. She'd managed to convince him to leave it behind when he went to preschool, but when he was home, the blanket was never far out of reach.

Jenny knelt down on the rug beside him. "What's the matter, honey? Not feeling very well?"

He looked at her, his eyes watery and slightly glazed. Very slowly, he moved his head from side to side. She feathered her fingers through his hair, brushing them against his forehead. It was definitely warm, bordering on hot. Just to make sure, she pressed her lips against it, employing the mother's tried and true thermometer. Cole shrank back and it hurt her heart, but she ignored the feeling.

"Definitely hot. I'll give him the Tylenol, Sandra." With a sigh, she rose to her feet. So much for Cinderella and her night out. "Looks like I won't be needing you tonight after all."

Sandra didn't usually come over on the weekends, unless Jenny found her caseload so overwhelming that she had to go in to the office on a Saturday or Sunday. But she'd made arrangements with the sitter to watch Cole while she and Eric went out. She hadn't made a big deal about it, but she had a feeling Sandra suspected what it meant to her.

The older woman looked surprised. "But what about your date?"

There was no use lamenting over it. She knew

what she had to do. Cole's welfare came first. She couldn't enjoy herself if she was worried about how the boy was doing.

"There'll be others." *When hell freezes over,* Jenny added silently.

Sandra saw through the act. "But you never go out," she protested. "I can stay with him, Miss Jenny. I promise I will call you if something happens. Kids, they get sick all the time."

Jenny was grateful to the sitter. She knew what Sandra was trying to do, and what she said was true, kids did get sick a lot, usually at the worst possible time. That didn't change anything. She couldn't just go off and leave Cole, couldn't think only of herself. What if what he had did take a turn for the worse, become something really serious? She was supposed to be his mother now. Mothers didn't desert their children to go and kick up their heels, no matter how infrequently those heels got kicked.

She vividly remembered how she'd felt that time when she was about ten and suffering from a miserable bout of the flu. Her parents had gone to some gala affair or other, leaving her with the housekeeper to watch over her. She'd secretly wanted her mother to stay, to be motherly for a change, and had felt miserably abandoned, even though she was probably closer to the housekeeper at the time than she was to her mother.

She wasn't about to run the risk of having Cole feel that way.

And if, in some deep recess of her being, she

was somewhat relieved that the matter of facing a date with Eric had been taken out of her hands, that her fantasy wouldn't die an ignoble death tonight when things didn't turn out to be as perfect as she'd always hoped they would, well, that was something she wasn't going to explore, other than to think that perhaps things did turn out for the best after all.

"That's all right," she assured Sandra. Picking up Cole, she bundled him up in his blanket and carried him to her room. She slipped the boy into the king-sized bed, drawing the cover over him. "This was just a charity thing anyway."

Clearly confused, Sandra looked at her. "I don't understand."

Jenny sighed. She was tired and disappointed and, most of all, concerned about Cole.

"Neither do I, really," she confessed. Making sure the boy was tucked in, she moved a chair into place beside the bed, just in case he moved to the edge and was in danger of tumbling out. Turning around, she placed a hand on the baby-sitter's arm and escorted her into the living room. "Go home to your family, Sandra. And thank you. I'll take it from here."

Sandra left several minutes later, under protest and continuing to volunteer to remain, until the door was finally closed and she was on the other side of it.

This is for the best, Jenny told herself again. This way she could still hang on to her fantasy, still pretend that Eric would suddenly become enchanted with her and that there would be no pockets of awkward silences, no desire on his part to get home and have the evening over with.

Squaring her shoulders, she went to the medicine cabinet. With any luck, Cole's fever would be gone by morning.

He'd pulled out all the stops.

Ordinarily, Eric liked being spontaneous, waiting for the moment to dictate the course of events, but for tonight, he'd pressed the family limousine driver into service, made reservations for two at the most exclusive restaurant in the city and had secured tickets to a musical that was sold out for the next six months.

He wasn't doing it to impress Jenny, but after all, this was his best friend's sister. From what he'd gathered from Jordan, Jenny hardly ever got a chance to go out. She was entirely about her work.

After being in her company for that short duration at the courthouse, he could well believe it.

She and Peter had a lot in common, he thought as the chauffeur came to a stop before Jenny's apartment complex. Maybe he'd see about trying to get the two of them together sometime.

His mouth curved as he got out. If nothing else, they could discuss their obsessions.

Eric was several yards away from the limo when he suddenly remembered and doubled back. He'd left her box of long-stemmed roses in the car. After taking the box out, he hurried up the stairs to her door.

He rang the bell twice before the door finally opened. Then his mouth dropped open, and for a second, he was rendered speechless.

"Did I get the date wrong?" he asked a minute later, his eyes sweeping over her. "Or have you decided to be incredibly casual?"

Instead of being dressed up for a night out on the town, she was wearing a blue and white plaid workshirt and jeans. He noticed that the jeans were hugging curves he hadn't been entirely sure she possessed.

There was obviously more to Jenny Hall than first met the eye, he thought, finding himself rather pleased.

Jenny couldn't stop the thought from forming. He looked gorgeous, simply gorgeous. It killed her to have to say what she did. "I'm afraid there's been a change in plans."

"Oh?"

Belatedly, realizing that she was keeping him standing on the doorstep, Jenny opened the door farther to allow him to cross the threshold.

"I tried to call you to head you off," she explained, "but I didn't have your number and you're not listed. And Jordan's not picking up his cell." Which was not all that unusual when it came to her brother. Jordan only answered his cell phone about half the time. The rest of the time his cell was off or the signal wasn't getting through, or, more likely, he was occupied and didn't want to be disturbed. "I'm really sorry about this."

Jenny's apartment was small and cozy and not like anything he'd pictured, Eric thought. People in his world lived in houses. Big houses, usually filled with antiques or overly expensive toys that pointed to their station in life.

He wondered if Jenny had taken some kind of vow of poverty.

Still holding the box of roses, he turned back around to look at her. "Is anything wrong?"

Without realizing it, she caught her lower lip between her teeth before saying, "Yes. I can't go with you tonight. Cole has a fever."

"Cole?" Was there a man in her life, after all? Someone her brother didn't know about?

Jenny nodded. "My son."

"Your son?" Eric echoed, dumbfounded. Obviously there were more than a few details Jordan had left out. He'd never mentioned that his sister was married before. "I didn't know you had a son."

He was looking at her so intently, Jenny flushed. "Cole's my godson, actually."

Well, that made a little more sense. At least it explained why Jordan hadn't said anything about the boy. But if this Cole was her godson, why had she just called him her son?

Eric made a stab at clearing this up for himself. "And you're watching him for the weekend?"

She shook her head. She wasn't making herself

clear. But then, just looking into those beautiful chocolate eyes of his had her brain getting all muddled.

"For the rest of his life," Jenny corrected, "or for as long as he lets me." She could tell by the expression on his face that Eric was still very much confused. "I adopted Cole."

In his opinion, the woman appeared to be bucking for sainthood. It was all well and good to adopt a child when you were married; after all, his parents had done it not once but three times, but taking on the responsibility when you were single was something else again.

"Where's his mother?"

In response, Jenny stood back and spread her hands wide before her.

"You're looking at her." And then she elaborated quickly, "His real mother, Rachel, worked in my office. We became friends." She didn't add that that was something that didn't happen to her too often. She didn't usually find people on the same wavelength as she was. "Rachel died of leukemia. Before she did, she asked me to look out for Cole." She anticipated Eric's next question. "Rachel was a single mother. Cole's father dropped out of the picture months before he was ever born."

The woman really did have a heart as big as all outdoors, Eric thought. In a way, she reminded him of his mother. "When did she die?"

"Six months ago." She still missed Rachel, missed

the talks they'd had. She tried to commit as many to memory as she could, wanting to tell Cole about his mother when he was old enough to understand. "Cole's had a rough time adjusting to the change. He's gone from being a happy, outgoing child to a sad, introverted one." She looked for understanding in Eric's eyes, knowing that most men wouldn't react well to being put in second place. "I don't like leaving him when he's sick. It came on suddenly," she added.

He vaguely remembered hearing or reading that a fever could come on suddenly with children. And leave just as quickly. Leslie Logan, while a concerned parent, had never made a big deal of their being ill. She saw to their comfort and made illness seem as natural as being well. They were never down for long.

"Have you called the doctor?"

She shook her head. She didn't want to come across as one of those nervous moms who called the doctor over every single little thing.

"I thought I'd watch him for a little while before I did that." Looking down, she finally became aware of the box Eric was holding. Long-stemmed roses by the looks of it. The man certainly believed in living up to his obligations, she thought. "I am really sorry about this."

"So am I." Although he certainly couldn't fault her for being a caring mother. "I had tickets for *One, Two, Three.*"

Her mouth dropped open at the mention of the

musical. That, too, had been on her wish list, although she knew she stood a far better chance of eventually seeing the play than she did of ever going out with Eric Logan. And here it all was, in one great big bundle. And she had to say no to all of it.

"But that's sold out."

A smile curved his mouth, torpedoing her stomach. "I know the producer."

Of course he did. He and his family probably knew everyone worth knowing. Probably so did hers, if she bothered to learn about their connections. She just never went that route.

Jenny tried to face the matter philosophically. "It's a shame to waste the tickets. Is there anyone you can call to go with you?" She thought of Lola. The woman had fronted the bidding, doing Jenny a good deed. And Lola had looked pretty interested in Eric herself. Maybe this was just fate, setting things right, she thought. Jenny crossed to the telephone in the kitchen. "I have Lola Wilcox's number if you—"

He was ahead of her, blocking her access to the wall phone. "I can call my own numbers," he assured her. Putting down the box on the kitchen table, he took out his cell phone. "By the way," he nodded toward the box, "those are for you."

She didn't feel right about accepting them, not after throwing a wrench into his plans like this. He'd obviously gone to some trouble to make arrangements, even if it had been easier for him than for most. But neither did she want to refuse them. She'd never received roses before. And these were roses from Eric. Never mind that he was probably just doing this by rote. She wanted them.

She decided to justify taking them by regarding the flowers as a consolation prize.

Opening the box, she looked down at plump, pink roses, nestled against deep green tissues, with sprigs of baby's breath mixed in between. She could feel something tugging at her heart. Jenny struggled to rein in her reaction. "They're beautiful."

Pressing several numbers on his cell phone, Eric nodded in response. He was calling another woman, just as she'd suggested. That it hurt watching him was something she'd forgotten to anticipate. Someone else would be sitting in the seat meant for her, enjoying the play. Enjoying his company.

She shut the scenario out and tried not to pay attention to what he was doing as she moved toward the far cupboard above the counter. She got out the vase she'd stored there. The vase that had contained flowers from her mother for her last birthday.

Jenny ran the water extra hard, trying not to listen in on his conversation. She disliked the person on the other end of the line on principle.

"Great," he was saying as she finally shut off the water. "The limo'll be by in a few minutes." Eric flipped his cell phone closed and tucked it away into his pocket.

Just like that, she thought. The man could find a

date in less time than it took to run water for long-stemmed roses.

She pasted a bright smile on her face before turning to face him. Placing the vase on the table, she began arranging the roses in it.

"Line up a date?" she asked brightly.

"I found someone to make use of the tickets and the reservation." Picking up a rose, Eric began handing them to her one by one as she tucked them into an artful position.

She stopped for a second. "Reservation?"

"To Blackstone's," he clarified, handing her the next rose. "I didn't want you to go to the play on an empty stomach."

Blackstone's. People made reservations for that restaurant a month in advance. *God, it would have been so perfect,* she thought.

It took some doing, but she managed to maintain a brave face. "So, the evening's not a total loss for you." She pretended to look at her watch, but in reality, she saw only her wrist. "I guess you'd better get going."

He handed her another rose. "Why?"

She looked at the flower, not at him. "Because you still have to pick up your date and you might miss the beginning of the play if you don't arrive at Blackstone's until—"

He held up his hand to stop her. She had a tendency to talk fast once she got going, he noticed. What surprised him was that he found it amusing rather than annoying.

"I'm not going to Blackstone's or to the play," he informed her.

She looked at him, confused. "But you were just on the phone—"

"With my sister." He grinned at the confused look on her face. "I'm giving the tickets and the reservations to her. She and her friend are going in our place." He didn't know whether that friend was male or female, but it didn't matter. His sister knew how to have a good time, which was all that mattered. "But I do have to send the driver over with them." Handing her the last rose, he crossed over to the door. "I'll be right back."

She still didn't understand. The man's obligation was over. He'd created the perfect date and she'd had to pass on it. He was free to go home or wherever he chose.

"Why?" she wanted to know.

The unabashed question had him stopping with the door partially opened. Was he reading her correctly? "Are you telling me to leave?"

Horrified, Jenny quickly backpedaled. "No, but I thought you'd want to. I mean, since I can't go to the theater with you and—" Overwhelmed, she stopped and tried again, cutting to the heart of the matter. To the only thing that *did* matter here. "Are you telling me that you want to stay?"

His expression was utterly guileless and utterly charming at the same time. "Sure, why not?"

She could think of a thousand reasons why he wouldn't want to remain here with a sick child and a woman he was only marginally obligated to. But just this once, she was not going to argue for the defense. She was going to stand back and enjoy this very odd twist of fate.

At least, until she woke up and discovered that she'd dozed off in front of the television set, because this was as much of a fantasy as anything she'd ever dreamed up.

She shook her head incredulously. "If you can't come up with a reason, I am certainly not going to give you one."

He laughed and stepped out. It had started snowing lightly and he turned up his collar. "I'll be right back," he promised.

I'll hold you to that, she thought as she closed the door behind him.

Because hope sprang eternal and part of her did believe in the Cinderella story, mice and all, Jenny left the lock off.

Nine

When she heard the door opening again, Jenny swung around, half expecting some stranger to be standing in her kitchen.

In a way, she had to admit that she was stunned to see Eric crossing her threshold.

He was back. He'd kept his word. Moreover, he didn't look as if he'd thought better of the whole situation and was searching for a excuse to ease himself out of his impulsive offer to remain.

"You looked surprised to see me." His expression was amused as he crossed to her. "I told you I'd be back. I just told the driver to drop the tickets off with my sister and to come by and pick me up later."

That meant he had no getaway vehicle. He really

was staying, at least until whenever "later" turned out to be. Still, she felt obligated to protest. "You don't have to stay, you know."

His grin grew a shade wider, completely undoing her in the process. She could feel the butterflies in her stomach being prepped and outfitted on the runway. "Well, I suddenly don't have any plans for the evening and you look as if you could use the company."

He certainly had that right. Though she loved Cole dearly, there were times when being a single mother became incredibly lonely. "I could," she admitted. "But there's no need for you to ruin your evening."

Loosening his tie, he made himself comfortable on the sofa, then looked up at her, waiting for her to join him. "What makes you think it'll be ruined?"

It was more of a case of her knees losing their rigidity than her actually making a conscious effort to sit down. Jenny dropped into the spot beside him, perching on the edge. "This isn't exactly a substitute for an evening at the theater and dinner."

She made him think of a bird about to take flight. Did he make her that nervous? He certainly didn't mean to. "The key thing in an evening out is whom you spend it with."

That didn't exactly make her feel any more confident. Jenny had never thought of herself as anyone's first choice. Her mother, in her own unconscious but ever so belittling manner, had seen to that.

"Jennifer, I don't know what man is going to look at you if you don't try to make yourself at least a little more attractive." How many times had she heard that?

Eric shifted on the sofa so that his body was turned toward her and said, "As I recall, I signed on for an evening with you."

That wasn't strictly true. Was he just being nice? "As I recall," she corrected, "you signed on for an evening with Lola Wilcox."

One side of his mouth rose. The two women seemed to be worlds apart. From what he knew about Lola, the attractive socialite saw very little beyond her own mirror. "Somehow, I just don't see Lola Wilcox giving up third row center tickets to *One, Two, Three* to play nurse to a child, no matter how sick."

Neither did she, but to say so seemed catty. Besides, Lola had been part of the group who'd decided to bid on Eric for her. She felt honor-bound to come to the other woman's defense. "Lola doesn't have any children."

He pinned her with a look. That wasn't exactly the point. "Neither did you, I thought."

Jenny shrugged, looking away. It wasn't something she saw as the topic of discussion for Eric and Jordan as they met over their weekly handball game. Except for heated protests from her mother, which flared up every so often, like last week, for the most part she had slipped into the role of Cole's guardian and then mother quietly, without any fanfare. She'd wanted it that way. Her goal was to provide stability for the boy, not gain any accolades or provide an air of false martyrdom for herself.

"It wasn't exactly something that would make the evening news, even on a slow news day." Before he could make a comment, she realized what he'd just told her about the theater tickets. Her eyes widened. "Third row center?"

He grinned and then nodded. Third row center was the choicest spot in any theater.

She was really, *really* sorry that she was going to miss that. But even with the perfect theater tickets to go along with the perfect man, she still wouldn't have changed her mind. Doing the right thing exacted a heavy price sometimes.

"You do live a charmed life, don't you?" Jenny could only marvel.

He thought of the parties and the women. And the occasional soul searching at 3:00 a.m. when it all felt somehow false and shallow.

"For the most part," Eric allowed offhandedly. He looked at her. "And then I come across someone like you and feel guilty."

She didn't begin to understand what he meant by that. "Guilty?"

He nodded. "We have more or less the same background and you're some kind of avenging angel for the poor and downtrodden." He glanced over his shoulder toward the bedroom where she had Cole.

"With a touch of Florence Nightingale on the side. And I'm—" He spread his arms wide. "Eric Logan, playboy."

Was he putting her on? She couldn't picture him feeling this way. "You're a great deal more than that," Jenny protested with feeling. "You're VP of Logan Corporation's marketing department—"

He was accustomed to people trying to cull favor with him by flattering his every move, but he had the feeling that Jenny was being serious. Something within him warmed slightly at the show of support. "For which I have nepotism to thank."

She gave him a look that said he should know better. "Terrence Logan could never be accused of being a blind man. He knows what he has. He is also not a stupid man. You don't place incompetent people into important positions no matter how much you might love them," she said pointedly. "You place them there only if they can actually do the job. Besides, I've also heard that you give more than your fair share to charities." That she had directly from Jordan

She seemed so serious, Eric couldn't help being amused. "You do like to argue, don't you?"

Jenny shrugged. "It's the lawyer in me. If you believe Jordan, it's also congenital."

Eric made his own judgment call on that. "It suits you."

She wasn't quite sure she was following him. Most people had a few choice words for her when she dug in. Her mother called her hopelessly stubborn. She'd heard worse terms. What she had never heard was a positive comment.

He probably meant something else, she decided. "What does?"

"Arguing." He shifted, moving in a little closer. Completely evaporating all the air around her. "A light comes into your eyes when you argue. Your whole demeanor changes."

Eric smiled. Now that he really looked at her, Jenny Hall was really nowhere nearly as plain as he'd thought she was. Even in a workshirt and jeans, with no makeup and her hair tousled, there was something inherently attractive about her.

He thought of the way she'd been in the courtroom the one time he'd seen her there. "It's like you're empowered."

Had she really created that much of an impression on him, she wondered, or was he just teasing her? "You only saw me in court for a few minutes," Jenny pointed out. "And mostly that was the back of my head."

"But it was an empowered back of the head." Eric laughed.

The sound was infectious and she joined in. It was a moment and they were sharing it. Despite the fact that she thought she looked more like a chimney sweep, she felt like Cinderella with the prince.

He caught himself thinking that with laughter in her eyes, Jenny looked almost beautiful. More than that, he found that there were other things at play here, an attraction he couldn't quite explain. She was hardly his usual type and it wasn't as if he even thought of her as a woman in the same light that he'd think of, say Lola Wilcox or the last woman he'd gone out with. Mona Nixon had been the latest in a long line of rather empty-headed, vacant women, he thought. Women who knew how to have a good time because that was all they did.

His eyes swept over Jenny, taking measure. Studying her. Without thinking, Eric reached for her. "When was the last time you can remember having a really good time, Jenny?"

His fingers were feathering through her hair, creating havoc in the pit of her stomach. She had to remind herself to breathe without sucking in air. She certainly didn't want him to think she was having an asthma attack. "Does now count?"

The question surprised him. "We're just sitting here."

"Yes, I know."

And sitting had never been so wonderful, or so arousing. If her heart didn't stop hammering the way it was, she was in danger of it just popping out of her chest and landing on her lap like a beached tuna.

He hadn't expected her to be so honest, so unguarded. He found it incredibly sensual. Incredibly seductive. Two words, two sensations actually, he would have never associated with Jenny Hall.

But then, he wasn't infallible. And this was one case in which he seemed to have been very, very wrong.

Without thinking, going strictly on instincts, Eric cupped her cheek. The look of sheer wonder in her eyes created a pocket of excitement within him. He brought his lips down to hers.

Instincts and curiosity had brought him here. Something more powerful took over the moment that he deepened first contact.

It surprised him beyond words.

She surprised him beyond words.

Jenny tasted of sweetness, of something fresh and compelling. And completely arousing. He deepened the kiss a little further, reluctant to stop, unwilling to withdraw. Wondering where this would take him.

Taking hold of her shoulders, he drew her closer to him. The soft moan that escaped her lips hovered between them, driving him further, bringing the temperature of his blood up higher.

His arms went around her.

Oh, God, thought Jenny, it was happening. He was kissing her. Really kissing her. The room was in danger of spinning completely out of control. It had already plunged into total darkness.

Everything had.

Everything except for the red-hot kiss that was sizzling between them and was threatening to completely incinerate her.

Kissing him, being kissed *by* him was everything she'd ever thought it would be. And more. So much more. Jenny felt as if a latch to a door within her was being raised and any moment, all sorts of sensations, all sorts of emotions and feelings were going to come stampeding out just like the bulls on their annual run in Spain.

Any second, she was going to jump him.

The startling thought had Jenny abruptly moving back, taking stock before she was completely unable to. She didn't want to frighten Eric away. Heaven knew she was already frightening herself.

With effort, she drew her head back. It took even more effort to open her eyes. She was afraid that ultimately, this was all a dream.

It wasn't. He was right there, sitting beside her, his face less than an inch away from hers.

"Wow."

Again her honesty overwhelmed Eric. And that didn't begin to address the fact that the single word she had uttered very aptly described exactly what he was feeling at this moment.

"Yeah, 'wow.'" Truly there was no other word for it. Because the kiss he'd just experienced, steeped in innocence and just barely restrained passion, had come close to knocking off his shoes.

Jenny pressed her lips together, trying to think. Trying not to taste him and all his masculine tastes. Was he laughing at her? Mimicking her? Right now she was too dizzy to care, but she knew she would later.

Rising uncertainly to her feet, Jenny dragged an equally shaky hand through her hair, then took a step backward toward the bedroom. "Um, I'd better go and check on Cole."

He nodded, watching her as she retreated. Now there went living proof that still waters certainly ran deep. He hadn't expected to be rendered all but speechless by someone he had until just recently considered to be rather mousy.

But then, Eric reminded himself, he'd seen her in action, seen her before a jury in court. Anyone who can plead with passion professionally couldn't be a mouse privately. No matter how she represented herself.

For Jenny, thoughts of Eric and the way he could make her body temperature rise to new heights vanished the instant she walked into the bedroom. Cole had fallen asleep, but he was thrashing around on the large bed. His face was flushed. She placed her hand on his forehead. The fever had risen. Jenny frowned. She didn't like this.

The moment she'd made her promise to Rachel to take care of the boy, she'd devoured every child-rearing book she could get her hands on. She knew that children had a tendency toward high fevers, higher than an adult could safely withstand, and that these fevers could spike suddenly and just as suddenly go down.

But she still didn't like it, still knew that it could be dangerous for the boy. She decided she'd give it a little while longer, and then call the pediatrician.

The sound of the doorbell brought her out of the boy's room. Now what?

She entered the kitchen in time to see Eric paying off a deliveryman at the door. The driver was wearing a jacket with a logo that proclaimed him to be from Blackstone's. There were several large bags with the same logo clustered on the floor beside Eric.

Jenny joined him at the door, indicating the bags. "What's all this?"

Thanking the man, Eric closed the door and turned toward her. "Well, I thought that since you had to eat—even if you weren't seeing the show—I'd have the restaurant send over dinner." He picked up the bags and placed them on the kitchen table. "I hope you like what I picked."

She would have liked it even if he'd had an order of mud pies and worms sent over. Still, she looked at the bags dubiously. "Blackstone's doesn't have take-out."

He grinned, taking two foam containers out of the first bag and placing them on the table. "They do if you know the head chef."

She laughed and shook her head. The man could probably get blood out of a stone. "I hope you use your powers for good and not evil."

His eyes met hers. She felt her blood heating again. "Maybe you could teach me."

Jenny forced herself to move to the cupboard. If they were going to have dinner, they needed plates, glasses, dishes.

And she needed to stop playing statue every time he looked at her.

But any thought of dinner, intimate or otherwise, evaporated the next moment. They both heard the noise at the same time. It was a choking sound and it was coming from the living room. Jenny flew into the next room. Her heart caught in her throat.

Cole had come stumbling out of the bedroom, his eyes wide with panic, his forehead glistening with perspiration. His small hand was clutched at his throat as he was desperately gasping for air.

Jenny fell to her knees beside the boy. He looked frightened out of his mind. "What is it, honey? What's wrong?"

But he could only make noises, awful, guttural sucking noises. When she tried to take hold of him, Cole pulled away from her and began to run around the room, as if searching for some elusive pocket of air, air that was refusing to enter his lungs.

Eric caught her to keep her from falling. But as she started for Cole again, Eric drew her back, taking charge. "Where's your bathroom?"

His question echoed in her head. It took her a second to make sense of it. She pointed into the main bedroom. "In there. Why?"

Eric didn't answer. Instead, he grabbed Cole and quickly carried the thrashing child to the bathroom. He shut the door behind him, leaving her standing on the other side.

Jenny stared at the door. Why had he shut it? "Eric, what are you doing?"

Again, he didn't answer her. Instead, she heard the shower being turned on full blast. When she tried the doorknob, he ordered her to stop.

"Leave the door closed."

"Why?" she demanded. "What are you doing in there?" She felt completely helpless, standing here like this.

"I've got the hot water on," Eric told her. "He needs to breathe in as much steam as possible."

Jenny had her ear against the door, trying to hear Eric above the rushing water. "Steam?"

"To open up his passageway," he explained. She heard him say something to Cole, but she couldn't make out the words. And then he raised his voice again. "I think he has the croup. Shh, it's going to be all right, Cole. Slowly, breathe slowly. That's a boy."

"The croup?" she echoed. She'd only been through a mild stomachache with the boy and a minor cold that had been over within three days. Both had rendered him more listless, but had been nothing of this magnitude.

Willing herself to stop panicking, Jenny began to calm down. Things she'd read came back to her. She recalled reading about the croup. The onset was sudden and it wasn't usually life-threatening. But there were times when the passageway became swollen and children could choke to death if they panicked.

She laid her ear against the door again, trying to make out any sounds. The desperate sucking noises seemed to have stopped.

That was a good sign, right?

"Eric," she raised her voice, trying to sound as calm as possible so as not to frighten Cole any further, "is he all right?"

"He's beginning to breathe normally," Eric told her. Jenny slumped against the door, drained, grateful. She heard relief in Eric's voice and she thanked God he'd been here for Cole. "I'm going to stay in here with him a few minutes and make sure he's all right. Why don't you get in touch with his doctor and give him or her the details, see what else they want us to do?"

She'd already left the door and was dialing the pediatrician's answering service. The fact that Eric had said "us" didn't strike her until after she'd completed the call.

The bathroom door opened just as Jenny was hanging up the phone. Eric emerged out of the sopping room with the boy in his arms. Cole looked a great deal better than he had when he'd gone in. The fear had left his eyes.

Both man and boy were soaked to the skin.

"I think you'd better change him," Eric suggested. Jenny quickly took Cole from him. Eric wiped his forehead with the back of his hand. Every part of him was dripping water onto the floor. He watched her place Cole on her bed after kissing him. "What did the doctor say?"

"That you were right, he has the croup." Bundling Cole up in her comforter, Jenny stepped away for a second to get a change of bedclothes from his room. She returned quickly with a pair of pajamas with a popular cartoon figure chasing villains across a field of light blue. "I told him what you did and that Cole was breathing normally again." Working quickly, she changed the boy in less time than it took to mention it. "How did you know what to do?"

Eric scrubbed his hands over his face, brushing off the moisture. "I saw it on an old episode of *Happy Days.*"

She covered Cole with a fresh blanket, then picked up his wet clothes from the floor. She dumped them in the hamper. Television. She couldn't even picture him watching it. "You really do surprise me."

He thought of the kiss they had shared, the one that had been prompted by curiosity and sustained by something far more energizing. "You might say it's been an evening of surprises."

Taking the comforter, she spread it out over the back of the rocking chair she had in the room, then draping the sides as best she could so that it would dry. Only then did she trust herself to look at Eric again. The light gray suit was a dark gray now and was adhering to his body.

She shook her head. "You look like you've been walking in a swamp. There're some towels in the closet," she offered, pointing to the small closet just behind him in the tiny hallway. "But I think your suit's ruined. I owe you a new one."

He shook his head, absolving her of the debt. "Just as long as Cole's all right." He looked back at the boy now nestled in the large bed. Cole looked a great deal calmer than he had only a quarter of an hour ago. "Did the doctor say anything about bringing Cole into the E.R.?"

She'd asked the pediatrician the same question, ready to take off immediately. "I told him that Cole was breathing normally again. He seemed to think that the danger was over. He told me to give Cole some children's Tylenol and if he still has a fever by tomorrow morning, to call his service and he'd see him then." She caught her lower lip between her teeth. "Dr. Silverstein did say he wanted me to leave a vaporizer running in Cole's room overnight."

He saw the way she was chewing on her lower lip and made a guess. "You have one?"

"No." She'd never needed one herself.

He'd thought as much. Eric began to cross to the door. "You'll have one," he promised.

Hurrying, Jenny managed to place herself in front of him just before he could reach the door. "You can't go out like that. You'll catch your death."

He liked the genuine concern he saw on her face and heard in her voice. Placating her, he stepped back and took out his cell phone. "All right. I can call Bart from here."

"Bart?"

"My driver." He flipped open the phone. "I was going to ask him to find an all-night drugstore and get you a vaporizer."

Getting a towel from the closet, she handed it to him. His thoughtfulness touched her. "Thank you."

Using one hand to press a preprogrammed number, Eric used the other to towel his dripping hair. "Don't mention it."

Prince Charming, she thought, sparing him a glance before she hurried back to Cole, had absolutely nothing on this man.

Ten

The low hum of the vaporizer purred throughout the bedroom, filling all the corners with the sound. If she listened very hard, beneath that she could detect the even breathing. Exhausted by his ordeal, Cole had fallen asleep and was breathing normally again.

Jenny stood in the doorway, watching him, trying to untangle her own jangled nerves and assure herself that he really was all right. That it was safe to step into the other room.

After a few minutes, she finally withdrew, but she left the door open just in case he took another turn for the worse. She felt pretty confident that he was on the road to becoming well again, but she wasn't about to take any unnecessary chances.

Thank God for Eric, she thought again, walking out into the living room.

And then she stopped dead.

Eric had opened up all the containers from Blackstone's and had them arranged on the coffee table. There was a plate for each of them as well as utensils and two tall fluted glasses he must have dug up from her top shelf. A bottle of white wine stood waiting on their pleasure. It looked like an impromptu picnic without the tablecloth, or the ants.

"What's all this?"

He turned around to face her, pleased that he'd finished just in time. He would have liked to have had a couple of candles standing in the center, but he hadn't been able to find any. Funny, he thought all women liked scented candles.

"No sense letting the food go to waste."

She smiled and shook her head. The man completely disarmed her. But then, he'd done that from his first smile. "Are you for real?"

Opening the wine bottle, he poured a little into her glass, then his own. "My last physical seems to point to that conclusion."

She sat down on the sofa. Taking a seat beside him—she noticed he'd spread out a heavy bath towel on his side so that he wouldn't get the cushion wet—Eric handed her her glass. "You're being an incredibly good sport about this."

"I like leaving myself open to new things." Sampling the wine, he pronounced it good in his mind.

He thought of the sleeping boy as he set his glass down again. "Besides, it's a great high, being in the right place at the right time to put my TV trivia to use." He offered her a napkin before turning to his own plate. "Most of the time it just involves supplying the right name for some character in an obscure, long-defunct TV series."

"So you do this all the time, watch old TV shows?" Who would have ever thought he remained at home long enough to do that? It made him seem so human.

"It's not something I'm proud of," he deadpanned, then he winked and threw her stomach into an uproar. "But it's one of my weaknesses."

"Well, your secret's safe with me." She paused, debating the question that rose up to her lips. Now that they were talking like this, now that he had selflessly come to Cole's aid and ruined a suit in the process that would have had other men complaining loudly, she found that she was comfortable around him. Comfortable the way she wasn't around most men. The way she hadn't been around him up to a few minutes ago. "So what's another weakness?"

Resting his fork for a moment, he paused to look at her for a long moment. "Girls with incredibly beautiful blue eyes." The air had stopped circulating in her lungs again. She forced herself to take a breath before she became completely oxygen deprived. "Too much of a line?" he guessed.

She heard herself laughing as she held up her thumb and index finger, creating a tiny space between them. "Maybe just a little." And then her voice grew serious. "I wouldn't think you'd need lines."

"Not usually." Realizing how pompous that must have sounded, he was quick to add very matter-of-factly, "Oh, it's not any fabulous charm on my part, it's the family name. Once women realize I'm part of *the* Logans instead of just some stray person with the same last name, they're pretty much won over."

She'd detected something in his voice. "And you don't like that."

No, he thought, he didn't. Didn't like the restriction it placed on him. "Doesn't give me a chance to know if they're attracted to me, or to the family fortune."

Her laugh was short and dry. "Although the money never hurts, I think it's a pretty sure thing that it's you."

There was something about the expression on her face, a genuineness that had him glad he'd decided to spend the evening with her rather than just going away. "And what makes you say that?"

Jenny's eyes widened. Did the man even know what he looked like? Men as good looking as Eric could write their own tickets. "Do you own a mirror?"

As her own words echoed in her head, Jenny retreated. She was being far too open and honest with him for her own comfort. The man probably thought she had a crush on him. That was something she would have died rather than to let him know. The last thing she wanted was for him to pity her.

Reaching for his glass again, he took a sip then set it down. When he did, he was grinning at her. "You're turning pink on me again."

Embarrassed, she looked away. "Sorry, it's a congenital thing, along with inserting my foot into my mouth periodically."

His finger crooked beneath her chin, he brought her face around so that he could look at her. "I'd like to see that."

She shrugged. "Figure of speech."

"It's also a lie."

He saw her eyes widen. She did have incredibly blue eyes, he thought. The kind of eyes a man thought about getting lost in. And now that he studied her so closely, he realized that she had a very attractive facial structure. Jenny's cheekbones came up high, giving her a rather sexy, haunting look.

"The woman I saw in court the other day doesn't sound capable of foot insertion." And then he laughed. "Unless it's into the other guy's posterior."

She felt the pink glow within her growing. Outside of an occasional kind word from Jordan, people normally didn't flatter her, not unless they wanted her to do something for them, or chair something.

Jenny felt it was safer to lower her eyes. Looking at him kept making her lose her train of thought. Kept making her return to the kiss that she'd wished had gone on forever. "Thank you. But that's another me."

"You have a clone?"

The amusement in his voice tickled her. "No." Jenny laughed. "It's just when I get caught up in something I think is a basic injustice, a whole other side of me comes out."

He nodded, as if understanding. "Like the Hulk, except prettier and not green," he supplied.

"Something like that." She wanted to get the conversation off her and onto something else. Anything else. She nodded at her plate. "This is excellent, even cold."

He knew what she was doing, but he played along. Besides, it was true. The food at Blackstone's knew no competition. Although tonight he hadn't taken that much note of the food. He'd finished his own serving without even realizing it.

"That's how they earn their reputation." Eric looked at the sofa. Even though he'd placed a towel over it, the spot he was sitting in was growing progressively more damp. And sitting beside her like this, talking like two old friends, had him entertaining thoughts that one didn't about one's best friend's sister. It was time for him to leave. "I think I'd better go before I wind up damaging your sofa."

She would have been willing to sacrifice a dozen sofas to have him remain even five more minutes, but from his point of view, she was sure he felt as if he'd put in enough time. More than enough time.

Jenny rose to her feet as he got to his. "I'm really sorry the evening turned out this way. You were probably looking forward to seeing the play."

"I've seen it." He saw the surprised look on her

face and guessed correctly at the question that came to her mind. "I got the tickets because I thought that you might enjoy seeing it."

He had a marvelous ability to understate something. She would have enjoyed standing on the corner, if it meant being next to him, breathing in the same air that he was. "I would have."

"And don't be sorry," he told her. He took her hand in his and held it for a moment. "I like unusual evenings."

Embarrassment fought to regain ground but she held it at bay. "Even if they mean ruining your suit."

He looked down at it. "It's not like this is my only one."

"Still, I feel I owe you one." It was the least she could do, she thought. After all, he'd refused payment for the vaporizer.

Still holding her hand, Eric waved away her words with his other. "I had a nice time."

She felt her heart skip a beat in response. But he was just being nice, she reminded herself. A smile entered her eyes. "Liar."

"No, really."

He watched the smile bloom in her eyes before it reached her lips. Felt himself becoming captivated. He ran the back of his hand along her cheek, an excitement tiptoeing quietly through him, taking possession before he even realized it was there.

He leaned over and kissed her.

Meltdown was immediate. There wasn't even a

second's hesitation. Jenny surrendered herself to it. She threaded her arms around his damp neck and cleaved to his damper chest. The wetness didn't matter. She figured there was enough heat being generated inside of her to dry off a rain forest.

This, she thought, was perfect. Far better than any play, any dinner at an exclusive restaurant. Just this sensation that was roaring through her like a runaway freight train. To save for the rest of her life in a small, airtight box.

A moment later, she stepped back, untwining her arms, trying desperately to scramble back to reality before she completely lost all sense of direction. She pressed her lips together, savoring the taste of him.

"Thanks for being here. I really don't know what I would have done without you and the Fonz."

Eric picked up on her mistake immediately and smiled. "Chachi."

"Excuse me?"

"Chachi was the one who knew enough to pull the kid into the shower. Joannie was baby-sitting. It was their first real date."

Staring at him in wonder, Jenny couldn't help laughing. Never in a million years would she have guessed that Eric knew this kind of trivia. "You really do get into it, don't you?"

Opening the door, he placed his finger to his lips, his eyes on hers. He forced a serious expression to his face. "That's our secret, remember?"

She nodded.

Jenny didn't slide bonelessly down on the floor until she'd closed the door behind him and was leaning against it.

The small, angular woman ran her long, thin index finger down along the day calendar on the side of her desk and frowned, shaking her head.

"I don't see your name here." She looked up at Jenny over the rims of her half-glasses. "You don't have an appointment." It was an accusation.

Jenny sighed, shifting the garment bag. The hanger was beginning to cut into her fingers. "No, I don't need an appointment." She nodded at the bag. "All I want to do is leave this with you."

Sitting at her desk like a gorgon, the secretary eyed the garment bag dubiously. Her small, tight frown became tighter. "For Mr. Logan."

"Yes." She had no idea that Logan Corporation hired the mentally challenged and placed them in such high positions. She'd stopped here on her way to court and she hadn't anticipated doing verbal battle with a female dragon. "If you'll just tell him that Jenny Hall said thank you, he'll understand."

The words seemed to have no impression on the woman. "Is he expecting this?"

"No." She certainly hadn't called Eric ahead about this, knowing he would only tell her again that it wasn't necessary, but she had told him before he'd left her apartment that she owed him a suit and she damn well intended to give it to him. "But—"

The woman blocked out any further explanation. She'd obviously heard enough. "Then I'm not sure I can accept this in his name."

Jenny was determined to leave it here for him. Ignoring the woman's protest, she draped the black garment bag over the back of the chair that was facing the secretary's desk and began backing away. This argument was eating into her time and she didn't have very much more left to spare.

"Accept it in whoever's name you want as long as Eric Logan eventually gets it."

Annoyed at being overridden, the secretary was on her feet, ready to grab the item and thrust it back to her. "I really can't—"

Exasperated, Jenny reached for the garment bag first and unzipped it with one fast jerk of her wrist. "Look, it's a suit, that's all. See? A suit."

She'd badgered Jordan for Eric's size. He only gave it to her after she'd given him all the details about Saturday night. She was surprised that he even knew about her date with Eric, but then, the two men did talk so she supposed Eric must have mentioned it to him.

Jenny pulled the zipper down farther to show the annoying woman that there was nothing else hiding within the bag.

"I accidentally ruined his suit Saturday and I just wanted to replace it." Yanking the zipper up again, she stepped back. She couldn't stay here and waste any more time with this woman. "Just see that he gets it, all right?"

"What was your name again?" the woman called after her departing back.

"Hall," Jenny called out, not bothering to even look over her shoulder. She was already at the threshold of the outer office. "Jenny Hall."

Jenny began to walk quickly toward the bank of elevators at the far end of the corridor. She was parked in a twenty-minute zone and the secretary with the heart of stone had already eaten up most of it.

She'd only gotten halfway to the elevators before she thought she heard him call her. Eric. She dismissed it as purely wishful thinking on her part and took another couple of steps before she heard him again.

This time she did turn around. Mostly to prove herself wrong, partly to hopefully prove herself right.

The next second he'd caught up to her. As if afraid that she might bolt, he took hold of her arm, anchoring her in place.

As if she could voluntarily move, she thought.

"How's Cole?"

She felt herself smiling at the question. "He's fine, thanks for asking."

"What are you doing here?" She looked a little flushed again, but this time, he knew he had nothing to do with it. "Another auction?" He'd heard her voice as she'd called out her name, but he hadn't left his office in time to see her.

"No, you've already done more than enough in the name of charity," she assured him.

She noticed that while her pulse was still scrambling, it was no longer threatening to leap out of her skin. Instead, it allowed a very nice, mildly invigorating sensation to flow through her veins.

"I just wanted to drop off a suit to replace the one you ruined at my place on Saturday. Saving Cole's life," she tacked on in case too much had happened between then and now for him to remember. She half expected him not to remember. She was sure there were far more memorable evenings in his memory bank.

"Nothing any other superhero wouldn't do," he quipped. She was back to her formal wear, he noted. Her hair was up, the two-piece black-and-white suit she was wearing beneath her opened coat was almost austere. No one would guess at the curves that were beneath it. The thought that he was among the few who did know that pleased him. "But I told you that you didn't 'owe' me a suit. You didn't have to go through all that trouble."

"And I told you that I'd replace it," she reminded him. "And I always keep my word."

He liked that. Liked a woman who felt that her word was her bond. It was an old-fashioned sentiment, but he'd discovered that sometimes the old-fashioned things were best.

"So do I," he told her. "We still have a date to go on."

She didn't want him to feel obligated. Neither did she want him to think that she'd showed up here to make him feel as if he now owed her something.

Jenny shook her head. "I don't think you understand. You put in your time, Eric. You're off the hook."

That was an odd way to put it, he thought. Had something he'd done made her think that he felt he was trapped into this? He was asking her because by no stretch of the imagination could Saturday have actually been called a date and because he found that he really did want to go out with her. She wasn't the usual type of woman he ran into and she intrigued him.

"And I don't think you understand while it was interesting and it let me get to know you under very adverse circumstances, Saturday night didn't really qualify as a date. I still need to take you out."

She tried again. "I absolve you of your debt."

He looked at her for a long moment, his gaze sweeping over her face, coming to rest at her eyes. "Maybe I don't want to be absolved."

"Oh."

Like a hard, weighted entity, the air stopped in her lungs. Eric couldn't be saying what she thought he was, what she wished he was. That would mean that he actually wanted to be with her. And, given his lifestyle and the kind of women he was accustomed to going out with, she couldn't really convince herself that he was truly interested in going out with her.

Maybe it had to do with some kind of code of honor. He was supposed to take her out so he was going to, no matter what.

Or maybe his mother had somehow gotten wind of what had transpired on Saturday. Staying home with a sick child would have certainly made points with the likes of Leslie Logan.

The more Jenny thought about it, the more likely it seemed. Leslie Logan was probably behind this, urging her son to "do the right thing and live up to his commitments." And right now, living up to his commitments meant taking her out.

What was she doing? Trying to talk him out of something she really wanted him to do? Jenny regrouped and approached the situation from the opposite end.

"Well, if you're really sure you want to do this," she said slowly, leaving him plenty of space to jump in and take the way out that she offered.

The more she resisted, the more he found himself wanting to go out with her. Women did not play hard to get with him. Most of the time the complete opposite was true. He had to fight them off.

Jenny was different and he found himself liking that difference. "I'm really sure I want to do this. When's a good time for you?"

Busy absorbing the sensation his words created along her skin, it took Jenny a moment to think. Several people passed them in the hall, glancing curiously in their direction. She felt herself smiling. "How does next Saturday sound?"

She knew that by suggesting Saturday, she made it clear to him that she had no social life, that every

Saturday evening was up for grabs, but she saw no reason to attempt to be coy with Eric—even if she knew how to manage the deception, which she didn't. As far as she could determine, she'd been created without a single coy bone in her body.

Since she had suggested the following Saturday, Jenny half expected him to demur, to say he had a heavy date, but to her surprise, without consulting any calendar, whether in his office or on his Palm-Pilot, Eric told her, "It sounds fine. Shall we make it for six?"

"Yes. Six," she repeated.

"I'll see you then."

Jenny nodded. She didn't clearly remember taking the last few feet to the elevator.

Eric could have named any time he wanted, and she would have found a way to be ready.

And this time, she promised herself as the elevator car arrived, she was getting to that store to buy something if not seductive, at least eye-opening.

The hell with eye-opening. If she couldn't be drop-dead gorgeous, at least her dress could be.

It occurred to her as she stepped into the car and had the elevator doors shut Eric out of view that she didn't know the first thing about buying a drop-dead gorgeous dress.

But there was one person who did.

Eric, she thought, pressing the elevator button marked Lobby, was going to be responsible for making her mother a very, very happy woman. She had been waiting twenty-six years to take Jenny shopping.

It looked as if the woman was finally going to get her wish.

"The day, Mother," she whispered under her breath, "has finally arrived."

Eleven

Is that really me?

The question echoed in Jenny's brain as she stared at the woman in the mirror. The woman who had evolved after an entire day's worth of work by a team of people who dedicated themselves to beauty and collected their weekly paychecks from The Body Beautiful Salon.

Jenny had trouble assimilating the image before her and reconciling it to herself.

She'd always felt so plain, so forgettable. She was completely convinced that she could move through a room filled with people and no one would even make note of her passage.

It was different now. Now she was fairly certain

that dead men would sit up and take notice of the woman in the mirror.

Her scrubbed and freshly peeled face looked vividly alive, thanks to a makeup artist who had put in ten years on Hollywood sets before coming to work for her mother's favorite exclusive salon.

The belief at the salon was that in order for the woman to shine, each part had to be addressed separately. She'd been massaged, molded, pampered and sweated. Her hair had been frowned over, shaped, highlighted and finally, after hours of deliberation and work, pronounced good.

The only thing Andre, the owner of the salon, had said that did not give them pause was "that darling figure you've got under those awful, awful clothes, sweetie. Why are you hiding it?" he had demanded. Not waiting for an answer, he had sent his assistants back into the other end of the salon, the area devoted to the sale of clothes that most women only fantasized about, and told them to return with no fewer than twenty selections.

That number kept growing over the course of the day. Andre and her mother, there every refining, excruciating step of the way, had rejected over a hundred before the ordeal was finally through.

But it was worth it.

There she stood, radiant from the top of her lightly sprayed hair to the bottom of her sinfully overpriced shoes, a vision of beauty.

Even her mother had said so. Not in so many words, but by her absence of criticism.

"Voila." Andre came out from behind her, much like a twenty-first century Merlin who'd put in extra effort to accomplish what he'd set out to do. He glanced at her exhausted mother who was sitting with a little less than perfect posture in the Louis XIV brocade chair. With a flourish of his hand, he indicated Jenny. "I give you the silk purse."

Meaning she'd come in as a sow's ear, Jenny thought. But she was far too pleased with the end result to take offense at the comment.

I'm pretty, Mother. I'm really pretty. Your genes weren't wasted. They didn't run out with Jordan.

Elaine slowly rose. Jenny glanced at her in the mirror. She'd never seen her mother looking more pleased. There was actually a satisfied smile on her face. The smile was for the salon owner, who was dramatically wiping his forehead.

"You've done very well, Andre."

"Very well?" he sniffed at the skimpy compliment. He raised himself up to reach his full five foot seven. "I have outdone myself."

Elaine nodded. "Yes, yes, outdone yourself," she echoed tolerantly. It was a consensus that the man needed no help feeding an already oversized ego. "Send me the bill for all of this."

Jenny's radar was immediately up. At all costs, she wanted to maintain her independence. It was bad enough that she'd had to ask her mother for help; she certainly wasn't going to allow her to pay for this day of vanity, as well.

"No, send it to me," Jenny insisted.

Elaine shifted her eyes to her daughter and tried hard not to be condescending. "Trust me, dear, you don't want to see this bill. I doubt if you make in an entire year what today has cost." Jenny opened her mouth, but her mother waved away the words. She didn't want to hear any of it. "I know all about your scruples and your independence, Jennifer, but I have been waiting for this day for twenty-six years now and I certainly don't mind paying for it."

The small smile on Elaine's lips widened just a tad. And deepened. It became more genuine, entering her eyes as they washed over her only daughter. "You do look lovely. I always knew it."

"It was," Andre was saying to them, attempting to draw the spotlight back where it belonged, on him, "a magical experience."

With a barely suppressed sigh, Elaine handed the man a folded hundred-dollar bill as a tip before proceeding down the line to the other personnel involved in this miracle of the salon.

All the way home Jenny had been afraid to breathe, afraid that somehow, with the wrong movement, the wrong turn of her head, she would somehow cancel out the magic. And she dearly wanted to retain it. For one night she wanted to be that princess, really *be* Cinderella.

She'd already felt the part before the fairy godmother came and transformed her. What she truly wanted was that special glow to enter her when she and the prince—in this case Eric—finally saw each other.

She wanted to knock his shoes and socks off.

But then, she reminded herself as she waited for the doorbell to ring that evening, Eric Logan was accustomed to gorgeous women. Women a lot more gorgeous than she was right at this moment. They populated his world, filled his evenings. If anything, she was going to be just another in a very long line.

She didn't care.

This was about one evening, one very special, magical evening in which she was going to willingly enter her parents' world and pull out every stop available to her. She wanted to make up for that first evening, show him that she could, on some small scale, compete with the kind of woman he was accustomed to taking out.

The look on her mother's face when she had dropped her off this afternoon said it all. Even Cole had looked at her with wide eyes, coaxing a glimmer of a smile from his lips. She was as ready as she was ever going to be.

Though she'd been waiting for it, when the doorbell finally rang, Jenny nearly leaped out of her well-oiled, lightly scented skin.

"That is your cue," Sandra told her. Jenny glanced over toward her and the boy. The woman gave her the high-five sign and mouthed, "Good luck."

Taking a deep breath, careful not to touch her hair, which was, as far as she was concerned, just perfect, Jenny opened the door.

"Hi, are you ready to—" The rest of the sentence evaporated like a drop of water falling on a hot radiator. Taken by surprise, Eric stared at the woman who opened the door. "Jenny?"

She tried very hard not to grin. "Yes?"

For just a moment he hadn't been sure that it was she. Not that there wasn't a resemblance between the woman in the doorway and Jenny, it was just that while Jenny was attractive, pretty even, this woman in the soft pink, strapless dress was absolutely gorgeous.

He couldn't pull his eyes away from her. "What did you do?"

She reached for her coat and purse. He automatically took the coat from her and helped her on with it. She noted with pleasure that he seemed to linger as he adjusted the coat on her shoulders.

"Gave my mother an early Christmas present." Jenny turned around to face him again. He was standing close again and the air within the small space had gone from normal to heated in an instant. "She's been dying to run amuck and make me over since the day I was born," she confided. Her mother's dissatisfaction with her had long since stopped bothering her, but Jenny had to admit that it was a pleasant change seeing approval in her mother's eyes this afternoon. "I've thwarted all her attempts—until now."

He stood taking her in. Enjoying the view. "What makes now different?"

She lifted one shoulder in a small shrug, not wanting to go into the matter too deeply. "I thought that since you were so nice about last Saturday, the least I could do was give you someone who looks presentable."

Was that what she called it? Presentable? The woman had a gift for understatement.

"You look a good deal more than just 'presentable,' Jen. You look beautiful. Are beautiful," he amended after a beat.

Her heart was pounding so hard, in a race it would have left a hummingbird far behind. She was hardly aware of taking her leave of Sandra, and just barely aware of kissing Cole good-night.

It occurred to her as Eric took her arm and escorted her to his fire-engine red Ferrari, that the man's eyes should be registered with the local police as a lethal weapon.

"Blackstone's?" Jenny asked as Eric brought the Ferrari to a full stop before the valet's station. He'd forgone having the limousine bring him tonight, telling her that he thought the evening deserved a more personal touch. She had to admit that sitting so close to him in the narrow vehicle certainly *felt* more personal.

The valet opened the door for her, helping her out. She made her exit just as Eric came around the hood, handing his key to the valet.

He took her arm, tucking it through his. They walked inside. "I thought you'd like to read the menu this time. Although you probably come here a lot."

"What makes you say that?" The dimly lit atmosphere embraced them the moment they walked in. Though large, the interior of the restaurant had a rich, intimate feel about it.

"So you can rub elbows with all the 'right people,'" he explained.

He didn't have to give his name to the maître d', she noted. The man nodded at Eric, then picked up two menus and led the way to a secluded booth.

Was this where he brought all the other women he saw? No, she wasn't going to spoil the evening by wondering about that, or by putting herself into a class she had no business being in. She wasn't really his date, she was, at best, an obligation.

The maître d' helped her with her chair, then politely backed away.

"That only comes into play when I'm trying to raise charitable donations," she told Eric. "There's no such thing as the right people, except maybe, the 'right one,'" she heard herself amending.

God, had she actually said that out loud? One afternoon with her mother and she was already brainwashed. It had to be subliminal suggestions. Elaine was good, she thought.

Not bothering with the lists of available wines, Eric paused to order a bottle for their meal. "You mean that 'special someone' mothers are always talking about and urging you to find?"

She laughed. For a split second they were both on the same side.

"You have one of those, too?" She thought of her mother and the uproar that ensued when Elaine discovered her plans to adopt Cole. "Mine was horrified when I took her up on the family part but neglected to bring a husband into the deal." Her face sobered slightly as she added in a lower tone, "She was very vocal about wanting me to place Cole up for adoption."

Since she'd opened the topic up, he decided to satisfy his curiosity about her. "Why didn't you? Someone else would have."

Maybe, maybe not, she thought with a shrug. "Someone else hadn't been there at his birth, hadn't given her word to a dying woman."

The waiter the maître d' had sent over brought the bottle of wine Eric had ordered. Placing a towel beneath its lip, the server poured first her glass, then Eric's before retiring the bottle and withdrawing into the soothing shadows.

Eric watched as the candlelight flickered across her cheek. He found himself wanting to trace its path. To touch her face. "And your word is important to you."

"Isn't yours to you?"

He liked the way she could dive into a serious conversation without either depending on her femininity or using it as a flag to wrap herself up in. She looked different when she was serious. The nervous look he'd come to expect faded and she was confident. Her own woman. He was finding himself more and more intrigued by this part of her.

"Yes," he replied, "but for most people, if the situation becomes inconvenient, they tend to forget the promises they made."

She took offense for Cole, then calmed herself. Eric hadn't meant anything by it. He was just paying lip service to something her mother espoused. "Cole isn't inconvenient."

He studied her over the rim of his glass, liking the passion in her eyes. The same passion he'd glimpsed in court. This was where she shone, in coming to the aid of the downtrodden, he thought.

However, tonight, with her looking the way she did, it was hard to remember that she was a force to be reckoned with in court.

"Still," he said thoughtfully, "it must be hard, being a single mother."

She thought of the last six months, of the uphill battle in trying to do her job properly and still not shortchange Cole. "Hard, but not impossible."

He had a feeling that even if it was impossible, somehow, Jenny would find a way to manage it. He was beginning to realize that away from the personal sphere, the woman did not know how to take no for any answer.

Dinner was wonderful. She could have lingered at the table for two all night. But that would have meant eventually needing the jaws of life to get her out of her dress, which left little room for expansion and showed no mercy to even an extra ounce.

Just as she placed her dessert fork down on her plate, she heard a soft, dreamy song drifting toward them, wrapping itself seductively around her.

Great, just what she needed. Something romantic to render her completely immobile. To further cause havoc with her nervous system, Eric leaned in over the table, looking somewhat contrite.

"I tried to get tickets for *One, Two, Three* again, but the producer's out of town, baby-sitting a new play that's opening in two weeks."

Her eyes narrowed slightly. "Are you apologizing?" As far as she was concerned, the evening was perfect. It had been perfect ever since she saw that expression on his face when he came to her door.

"Well, I had tickets for the play last week and you have every right to expect me to take you to it—"

Touched, she stopped him, placing her hand on his without thinking. "Dinner is more than enough."

He looked at her, trying to decide whether she was simply going through the motions, or if she was being serious. In either case, his feelings about the matter didn't change.

"For ten thousand dollars, you deserve more than dinner."

Maybe she shouldn't have allowed herself to be made over at the salon, she thought. Now Eric thought she was just like all the others, out to get something. But she didn't need empty trappings. "Coming to Cole's rescue absolves you of any 'debt,' real or imagined."

"I meant as a date."

She pretended to give it serious thought. Keeping a straight face, Jenny asked, "Okay, how are you at juggling?"

"Terrible," he deadpanned.

She grinned at him. "That might be worth watching, then."

The music was still infiltrating the dining area. The dance floor was closer to the small band. "I'm better at dancing."

I just bet you are. You're probably better than most mortal men at everything.

For a moment, she let herself fantasize about being in his arms. But when he turned her hand over and took it in his, alarms went off in her head. "What are you doing?"

"In order to dance, you have to first get up." He smiled at her, about to rise. "Going to the dance floor might help, too."

She disengaged her hand from his, dropping hers in her lap. "You don't have to prove to me you can dance. I'll take your word for it."

He looked at her for a long moment. "Don't you dance?"

There was no point in denying it. She couldn't even pinpoint how long it had been in years. "Not since my mother stopped forcing me to attend those awful cotillions."

"Then maybe it's time you did again." He took her hand again and this time brought her to her feet. "Don't worry, it's like riding a bicycle. It'll come back to you," he promised.

She found herself standing very close to him. Jenny absorbed the electricity that ran through her at the moment of contact, savoring it. It took her a moment to find her tongue.

"You're going to regret this," she warned.

She was a funny contradiction of courage and fear, Eric thought. She made him feel protective. That hadn't happened in a very long time. "I'll be the judge of that."

He led her to the dance floor. Turning around, he took her into his arms.

She struggled not to melt into them. The song was soft, sexy, the melody winding its way into her system. It had words, but they were just beyond her memory's reach. Her cheek resting against his chest, his cologne filling her senses, she stopped trying to remember and just went with the moment.

Going to see a play didn't hold a candle to dancing with him. Even the most desired, sold-out play in Portland.

Breathe, remember to breathe, she ordered herself.

But it was hard concentrating on anything except the feel of his arms around her. They were protective and hard. He was deliciously strong, she thought, wondering when he got the time to work out.

She heard him murmur something into her hair and she looked up. "Excuse me?"

He looked down into her eyes, his smile raising her body temperature several degrees. You'd think she would get used to that, she thought. But she didn't. "I said I'm not regretting it yet," he told her.

"Neither am I." It took an extreme amount of self-control not to sigh the words out.

Jenny watched the shadows ebb and flow within the interior of the car as Eric drove her home. The shadows mimicked the feelings going on inside of her.

So this was what Cinderella felt like after the ball was over, she thought. Within, her excitement was mingling with sorrow because it was the best evening she'd ever had, better than anything she could have cvcr hoped for. But it was all about to end.

Still, there was one wonderful, magical night to press in the pages of her memory. Something to take out and examine and hold to her chest whenever she was feeling down, she thought.

The car had stopped moving. Eric had pulled up into guest parking. They were home, she realized suddenly. Time for Cinderella to thank the prince. She turned to face him. "I had a lovely evening, Eric."

So had he, Eric thought. Moreover, he found himself unwilling to allow it to end just yet. "Why don't we continue it?"

She wasn't sure she understood just what he was saying. "Excuse me?"

There were times when he liked being completely impulsive. This was one of them. He played with a curl that rested against her cheek. "Fly with me to Vegas," he urged.

There was a roaring noise in her ear, and she had to strain to hear his voice above it. "Just like that."

He grinned. "Just like that." He ran the tip of his finger along her cheek again, making plans as he went along. "We can make a weekend of it. I've got a private plane standing by, it can get us there in less than forty minutes. I have a standing reservation for a suite at Caesar's Palace—"

Taking off at a moment's notice without a care to anchor her down. This was her parents' world. His world. But it wasn't hers, not anymore. For the space of an evening she'd forgotten about the path she'd taken.

But now, struggling against the very real temptation Eric was offering her, she reminded herself that there was more than just her to consider. She had responsibilities. Large ones.

"It sounds very tempting," she began.

He was already taking out his cell phone to call his pilot. "Good, then—"

She stopped his hand. "No."

For the moment, he let the phone slide back into his pocket. "No?"

She shook her head slowly. "I'm going to hate

myself for saying it again, but no." She backed up her reason quickly, before she lost her nerve and gave in—the way so much of her was begging her to do. "I have a summation to deliver on Monday. I've got to prepare for that. And there are two more cases waiting for me to get back to them. And, most importantly, there's Cole—"

He didn't mean that she should abandon the boy. "You said he was fine," he reminded her.

"He is, but I can't just up and leave him." Cole wasn't some stuffed animal to be left in the closet when she tired of him; he was a child with feelings and vulnerabilities.

"Of course not. I just thought that if I paid your baby-sitter—"

Again, she stopped him before he could continue. Because if he continued, it would all sound too seductive to her and she might give in. "That's very generous of you, Eric, but no." She saw the bemused way he was looking at her. "What?"

"I don't think I've ever heard a woman say that to me before." He stated the fact honestly, without any ego. It was a new experience for him, one that he couldn't say he liked exactly, but one he could respect.

She laughed self-deprecatingly. "Then I guess I'll stand out in your mind."

"You already did before you said no." He got out and rounded the trunk of his car. Taking her hand, he helped her out of his car. They walked in silence to her door.

When he brought her to the landing, she turned to face him and hesitated for a moment. "Would you like to come in for coffee or a nightcap?"

Amusement curved his mouth. "That won't interfere with anything?"

She could feel his smile weaving into her senses. "No."

"Then I'll have whatever you're having."

Okay, one meltdown, served hot, she thought, turning from him to unlock the door.

Twelve

Sandra sprang up from the sofa the instant the door was opened and they walked in.

"Ah, Cinderella is back from the ball. And she has brought the prince with her." Sandra nodded, well pleased. She tucked under her arm the book she'd been reading. "That is much better than keeping a glass slipper for a souvenir."

The woman was at the door before either one of them was even clear of it, her hand on the knob. She was obviously in a hurry to take her leave and clear the stage for whatever she thought might happen next.

"Cole went to sleep at eight." Her eyes briefly met Jenny's. "No nightmares tonight. See you Monday."

And then she was gone.

Eric looked at Jenny quizzically. "Nightmares?" At Cole's age, he'd been afraid of monsters under his bed and in his closet. Peter, he recalled, had been particularly kind to him during those times.

Jenny nodded. "Cole has them sometimes."

She began to slip out of her coat. Behind her, Eric helped her off with it, then held the coat out to her. Turning around, she took it and smiled up at him. This still all seemed like a dream, she thought.

"About his mother," she continued. Walking to the coatrack, she hung up the coat, then placed his on the hook next to it. "He misses her a great deal. But they're getting fewer, thank God."

She found herself looking up into his eyes. How had that happened? Jenny felt the foundation slipping out from beneath her feet. Taking a quick, fortifying breath, she redirected her thoughts to playing hostess.

"So, you never did say what I can offer you." She took five short steps back into the kitchen and then to the refrigerator. Opening it, she peered in. She wasn't set up for company. There were cans of soda, a container of orange juice and a half consumed bottle of wine, courtesy of her brother's last visit. "I'm afraid I don't have much of a selection."

"I don't need a selection. Quality has always been my criterion."

There was something in his voice that had her heart momentarily stopped before it launched itself back into high gear. Closing the refrigerator door, she turned and found herself less than an inch away from him.

The air became scarce.

“Define quality.” The question came out in a whisper instead of her normal voice. Anticipation was doing a number on her insides.

What did she expect to happen, a small voice within her head asked. That he’d whisk her into his arms and make mind-numbing love to her?

Expect? No. Wish for? Yes.

Eric was speaking, calling her back to the moment. “Something rare, something desirable,” he said. “Jenny?”

She moved her lips, forming the word. Whether it got out or was audible, she couldn’t quite tell.

“Yes?”

Very slowly, he tilted her head up with his thumb and forefinger. “I’d like to kiss you.”

Her heart was hammering so wildly, she was surprised it hadn’t launched itself out of her chest and smashed against his. “I’d like that, too.”

She saw the smile crinkle his eyes just a moment before he brought his lips to hers.

Explosions, beautiful and encompassing, went off in her head, brighter than any Fourth of July display she’d ever seen. Grasping his forearms, Jenny clung to him as if he was her entire universe, because, for this very small island of time, he was.

If she’d been a bell, Jenny thought, right now she’d be ringing. Loudly.

Eric held her to him, deepening the kiss inch by agonizing inch until a very strange thing happened to him. He fell in. Fell into the huge abyss he'd created, fell in and felt a wild exhilaration overtaking him that he hadn't expected. It was as if the sweetness he encountered had set fire to his blood.

He gathered her closer, so close that he felt he could absorb her completely. And even that wouldn't have been enough.

Something was happening to him that he was unfamiliar with.

The way she yielded against him excited him beyond words, surprising him beyond measure. By no means was he a novice at this, yet she'd set fire to him in a way he'd never before felt.

There was a purity about her eagerness that rocked him. This wasn't some jaded socialite after a good time. He wasn't with someone who could perhaps, with a minimum of effort, change partners if the mood and the incentive was just right. He was with someone who made him feel more than twelve feet tall.

Someone who made him feel as if she wanted *him,* not Eric Logan, not the Logan name or money, but him. Just him.

And he wanted her.

Cupping her face with his hands, Eric drew back to look at her for a moment, as if to see if he was hallucinating or if this woman who was creating such unforeseen havoc within him was really there.

Why was it the more he looked at Jenny, the more

beautiful she became? For most men, that was a side effect of drinking, but he was stone-cold sober. Her deep blue eyes looked dazed and there no longer was the hint of pink lipstick on her lips. Instead, the lines that defined her mouth were blurred, made that way by the imprint of his own.

He found that incredibly arousing.

Eric could feel his blood surging, could feel himself wanting her. He brought his lips down to hers again, trying to quench the needs, the urges, but succeeded only in feeding them, making them far greater than they were just a few moments ago.

The feel of her body against his aroused him, hardened him.

He wanted to go slowly, but he was afraid that if he did, she would draw away, unsatisfied. And equally afraid that if he went too fast, he would only succeed in frightening her away.

He didn't want to hurt her.

He didn't want this to end yet. He'd never felt like this before, never felt an urgency wrapped in caution before. And always before, he could pull away. Now, quite honestly, though he told himself otherwise, he wasn't all that sure he could do that.

But he knew he had to.

He couldn't force himself on her. Not if this wasn't what she wanted, too.

Feeling shaken, Eric drew back again to look at her, to search for his immediate future in her face. In her eyes.

Don't stop, she begged silently.

Was there something wrong? Why was he drawing back just when all the systems in her body were begging her to finally go forward.

Jenny took a deep breath, trying to steady herself. It didn't help. Her craving got the best of her. This time she kissed him, wrapping her arms around his neck and drawing him to her. He'd unleashed something within her, all the stored-up dreams and desires of a woman who had never felt safe enough to venture forth, never given herself to a man before. Never even been tempted before.

She was tempted now.

Hell, she was far beyond just tempted.

Because she knew that this time, it was different. This was Eric. The one who crept into her dreams, both day and night.

From the very first time she'd seen him, she'd known that he was the one. The one she wanted to make love with someday. But it had gotten to the point that she'd thought that day would never come.

And now here it was. She could feel it. Almost taste it. And she went with it, a little afraid, but predominantly wanting him. Wanting to finally feel what other women had felt—although a part of her doubted that anyone had ever felt quite this magnitude of passion before.

She moaned.

The sound went straight to Eric's gut, tightening it. He was running his hands along her sides, slowly, passionately, committing her contours to memory. The swish of the material beneath his fingers teased him.

He wanted more.

He wanted to feel her, feel her skin, run his palms along her breasts, her nipples, the flat of her belly. Wanted to savor her, to make her his.

The possessiveness stamped across his desires would have given him pause if he were thinking more clearly, but he wasn't. There was something about the taste of her mouth, the promise of her body, that had sent him beyond the realm of coherent thought.

The one thought that dominated him was that he wanted her.

Needed her.

At this moment in time, there was nothing more urgent than having her.

Finding the zipper on the back of her dress, he slid it down to its source, parting the dress from her body, his mouth still sealed to hers. And then, because some vague part of him could still function, could still think, though that was beginning to change fast, he picked her up in his arms.

"Your bedroom free?"

She sank into his arms as if she'd always belonged there.

"Yes," she breathed.

Yes, everything within her sang. He wanted her. She didn't care why, or that he had wanted so many others before her and would want more, after her, right now, he wanted her.

Perhaps even as much as she wanted him.

But it wasn't a contest. She'd already won the prize. And it was just getting better with each passing moment.

He brought her inside her room, then closed the door with his elbow. He was tempted to just have it slam, but there was a child on the premises and he didn't want to wake him. Or be responsible for introducing a lesson in life that the boy was far too young to learn.

Once the door was closed and he had stepped away from it, Eric set her down. Slowly he drew her dress away from her, taking care not to tear it, although that was exactly what he wanted to do to be rid of it. Jenny was wearing something provocative beneath. Something he would have said came from one of those catalogs that specialized in perfectly shaped women. Right now Jenny looked as if she'd stepped right out of its pages.

He could feel his gut tightening again and an ache beginning in his loins.

It took all he had to rein himself in, to go slowly. He'd never felt this level of urgency before. He wanted to rip the flimsy garment from her, not search for a clasp and undo it.

But search he did, undo it he did, until she was standing before him in nude perfection. He wanted her with every fiber of his being.

Standing there naked, Jenny thought she would have felt self-conscious. He was the first man to see her like this, the first man she wanted to see her like this. But none of her insecurities had taken hold. It was as if she was another person entirely. One who was comfortable in her sexuality instead of made to feel awkward by it.

In the next moment, Eric heated every part of her body as his hands passed over her. As she watched, her breathing grew more and more shallow until air finally refused to fill her lungs in any perceivable measure. Eric stepped back and stripped off his shirt and his trousers. But as his hand went to the waistband of his briefs, Jenny stopped him. The surprised look on his face gave her a strange sense of power. She reveled in it without understanding its origin.

Her hands on both sides of his taut hips, her eyes on his, she drew the black material away slowly, a half inch at a time. By the time she cleared the fabric to his thighs, he took over, yanking the confining briefs down the rest of the way and kicking them aside as he took hold of her, pressing her body to his.

Laying her down on the bed, he began to memorize the contours of her body, his fingers first sweeping along her soft skin before his lips did the same.

Jenny moved against his touch, sensitive to every nuance, desiring to feel everything. She twisted so hard against him that he felt as if the control he'd managed to maintain up to now was a heartbeat away from snapping altogether.

Finally, his head spinning, his blood surging, Eric couldn't wait any longer.

Positioning himself over her, his mouth sealed to hers, drawing in the taste of summer fruit, he spread her thighs with his leg and began to enter.

He felt her slight withdrawal, felt the resistance as he began to drive himself into her.

A vague alarm began to go off in his head, growing louder as the realization penetrated his brain.

He pulled his head back.

"Jenny?"

She could tell by his tone what he was going to say. What he was going to do. Or not do.

No, she wasn't going to have him stop, not now, now when she was so primed for him. Not when everything she ever hoped for, wished for, dreamed of, was within a breath away.

Closing her legs around his torso, she held him captive, drawing in the length of him.

The pain burst into her being, spreading out like a fire. She forced herself beyond it, concentrating only on the sensations to come, on the need for fulfillment. The pain passed.

Very quickly, she began to move her hips, coaxing him, tempting him until the rhythm between them exploded in heated earnest. It continued, growing steadily until suddenly it was the Fourth of July all over again, but this time it was to the tenth power.

A sensation she had never felt before exploded

over her, bathed her, anointed her. And when it finally began to withdraw, it left a euphoria in its place that cradled her in its arms.

She sighed, curling her body into his.

When he drew back, creating a pocket of air that chilled her down to the very bone, she felt suddenly deprived. Almost bereft.

Eric raised himself up on his elbow and looked at her. "You're a virgin."

Was he angry? Had her lack of experience offended him somehow? But he wasn't like that, was he? She tried her best to gather her courage together.

"Yes."

He felt as if he'd stolen something precious from her. If he'd known— But how could he?

"Why?"

For a moment, she didn't comprehend his question. Finally, she said, "That's the way the package comes, until it's unwrapped."

He blew out a breath, angry with himself. This shouldn't have happened. He should have brought her to her door and then gone home.

"No, you know what I mean." Impatience and annoyance echoed in his voice. "Why didn't you tell me?" he demanded.

"Because people don't come with disclaimers written on the sides of their body like a package of cigarettes," she told him. "You have to admit that there wasn't exactly much of an opening in our conversation for this kind of information."

"I just thought that you—" Frustration stole away his words, his very thought process. "How old are you, anyway?"

At this moment, she felt a great deal younger than her birth certificate indicated she was. "I'm twenty-six years old."

She was the same age as he was, Eric realized. But he was experienced and she was…she was an innocent, that was what she was. That was why she felt like purity in his arms. Because she was. And he'd robbed her of that. "Twenty-six and you never, um—"

"No, I never um-ed. I never even came close to um-ing," she answered honestly.

But she was pretty, more than pretty. And she was a Hall. Her family was rich. That meant she should have been in the social whirl. And yet, Eric reminded himself, she hadn't been. Still, it was hard to believe that a woman could reach her age and not have been with at least one man.

"Why?" he repeated again.

"Because I never wanted to." She pressed her lips together, touching his shoulder lightly with her fingertips. "Before tonight."

She was beginning to stir him again. Damn it, what was the matter with him? He'd just done something thoughtless and here he was, wanting to do it again.

Frustrated, he sat up and dragged his hand through his hair. "You should have told me."

His tone was accusing. He *had* been disappointed. She tried not to let it hurt too much. "And you would have stopped."

He looked at her over his shoulder. Damn but she looked tempting. He sealed in his resolve, but he could feel it leaching out again. "Yes."

She shrugged, her case evident. "That's why I didn't tell you."

Eric shifted around to look at her. How the hell was he supposed to make this up to her? "I feel like I robbed you of something."

Was that it? Jenny questioned. He felt guilty because he was her first? She was exhilarated because he was her first. And more than likely, her only. After what she'd just experienced, she couldn't see herself drifting into a lesser relationship.

She ran her fingertips along his spine, watching the muscles quicken as she glided them along his skin. "You would have only robbed me of something if you had stopped. I might hem and haw and turn pink at the most inopportune times," she allowed, "but I'm not the pushover you think I am, Eric."

She was driving him crazy. He twisted around to face her more squarely.

"I've seen you in court," he reminded her. "I don't think you're a pushover. But I do think I'm guilty of overwhelming you."

The smile he saw blooming in her eyes went straight to his gut. And spread out into his loins. He tried to latch on to some calming thought. But for the life of him, he couldn't force one into his head. She was filling up every space he had.

She raised her arms to him. "Care to overwhelm me again?"

Here he was, trying to find a way to make up to her for what he'd done and she was making him want to do it all over again.

"What?"

Because he was taking this far more seriously than she'd thought, Jenny decided to approach the matter philosophically.

"Well, you can't exactly recycle virginity and I'm not about to become a born-again virgin even if I never make love with you or any man again…so, if you find yourself so inclined—"

There was just so much temptation he could withstand. Eric lay down beside her again, drawing her into his arms. Somewhere along the fringes of his mind, it surprised him how right this felt, but it was only a vague thought in passing. "You are definitely not what you seem, Jenny Hall." He pressed a kiss to her throat.

"That's a relief," she sighed.

Laughing, Eric kissed her lips. And discovered that the second time could be even sweeter than the first.

Thirteen

He spent the night.

He hadn't intended to. Spending the night with a woman wasn't something Eric did with any sort of regularity. Especially not the very first time he made love with that woman.

But that, too, had been different this time.

Without him noticing, the hours had softly woven themselves into one another. He'd lost count how many times Jenny's heady mixture of innocence and sensuality had aroused him, had lured him into making love with her "just one more time." Finally, completely spent and exhausted, he'd fallen asleep. He had no recollection of the hour.

Daylight, rather than the soothing blanket of darkness, had made itself at home within the bedroom when he finally woke up. From the looks of it, as he began to pry open his eyes, it had been there for quite some time.

He had no idea how long the child who was looking down at him had been there.

Startled by Cole's presence, Eric bolted upright. For a second, his inherent charm deserted him. For the life of him, he had no idea what to say or do. A child had never been part of this sort of scenario for him before. But then, what had transpired last night between Jenny and him didn't exactly come under the heading of business as usual, either.

At least the boy didn't look upset at seeing him here in Jenny's bed. That was something.

"Um, good morning," Eric finally managed, then looked to be bailed out by the woman next to him.

Except that she wasn't next to him.

The space beside him was empty. And cool when he ran his hand over it. Jenny had obviously gotten up and left the bed without his waking up.

Leaving him to flounder here beneath the scrutiny of big green eyes.

And then, as he searched for something else to say to Cole, the boy smiled at him. Really smiled, as if he recognized him to be a friend.

"Hi."

"Hi," Eric echoed a little uncertainly. The entire time they had spent in the steam-encased bathroom together last Saturday evening, he hadn't heard a word out of the boy other than the initial gaspings that had sent him hurrying into the small room and running the shower water in the first place. "So you can talk." He needed bailing out. Fast. "Um, where's your mother? I mean…"

Eric's voice trailed off. What did the boy call her? Jenny? Ms. Hall? He probably didn't call her Mom. Or did he?

Lost, Eric wished he'd had the presence of mind to leave last night the way he'd initially intended. If he tried to analyze it logically, he still wasn't sure how he'd gotten here, to this point. Into this bed. Last night was a blur. A delicious blur.

All he knew was that one thing had just led to another. Very quickly it had become apparent to him that he wasn't going to be leaving. Not without making love to Jenny. The first time, he realized, he'd made love *to* Jenny, the second and all the times that followed he had definitely made love *with* Jenny. She was a fast learner.

"You're up." Alerted by the sound of voices, Jenny had come to investigate. And come to Eric's rescue.

He looked rumpled, she thought. Adorably so. The sight of him sleeping beside her had made her hesitate when getting out of bed this morning. But there was Cole to think of and she didn't remember how the four-year-old mind worked. She thought it best not to add to Cole's confusion by having him find Eric and her together in her bed. Especially since all she'd been wearing at the time was a very pleased smile.

She leaned her hip against the doorjamb. "So, how do you feel about breakfast?"

He looked up at Jenny. She looked fresher than a living human being had a right to in the morning. His eyes shifted back to Cole. "I think maybe I should get going."

She knew he was right, that she'd had him way longer than she ever dreamed she would, but yet, there was this reluctance to let him escape.

"It's already made," she told him cheerfully. "Most important meal of the day." Taking Cole's hand in hers, she drew the boy toward the doorsill. "Why don't we let Mr. Logan get dressed?"

Cole looked very solemn as he regarded Eric in the bed. And then he nodded his head, his intense green eyes shifting from Eric to her, but not before he smiled at him again. "Okay."

The smile was not lost on Jenny. It warmed her heart. Since his mother's death, Cole ignored most people. "He likes you," she told Eric. "I think you made an impression on him."

And Cole, Eric thought a few seconds later after Jenny had closed the door and he was hurrying into his clothes, had certainly made one on him.

He meant to just walk through the apartment to the front door, leaving a cheery "goodbye" in his wake. He never made it that far. The second he crossed their path, he was doomed.

Eric wound up staying for breakfast.

What made the argument for him was not so much the food, which he'd discovered she'd sent out for from the local family restaurant less than a mile away. The food was good, but not spectacular. What had kept him was the company. Especially Jenny.

Jenny seemed softer, more personally confident than he had come to expect, but far less aggressive than when he'd seen her in court. He thought of that old movie with Joanne Woodward, *The Three Faces of Eve.* One shy, one brash and one just right. He couldn't help wondering if this was the real Jenny, if he had made it past her two layers to get down to the heart of the woman.

He liked this version. A lot.

"More coffee?" Jenny poised the half-empty pot over his cup. For a man who'd initially claimed he wasn't hungry, he'd made short work of the French toast she'd served him.

Covering the rim of the cup, Eric shook his head. The coffee, she'd told him, she'd made herself. "Not that it's not good, but I might start sloshing as I walk to the door."

Eric noticed that while nibbling on his piece of toast like a tiny mouse husbanding a meal, Cole had been silently observing him the entire time he had sat at the table. Now that he was rising, Cole scrambled to his feet, as well.

Eric suppressed a grin. It was like having a three-foot shadow.

Jenny walked him to the door with Cole echoing

his footfalls. Eric turned to look at her. It was a domestic scene, something he'd never even had a mild interest in before despite all his mother's less-than-subtle hints about terminating his rootless, bachelor days. Yet somehow, he found it strangely appealing. He wondered if there had been something in the coffee.

Still, he found himself lingering at the door and heard himself saying, "I'd like to see you again."

He's being polite, nothing more, she told her leaping heart, ordering it to settle down. "You don't have to say that."

He tabled the urge to kiss her goodbye, not knowing how that might affect Cole. He already knew how that affected him. "Sure I do. How else will you know that I want to see you again?"

He's changed the word from like to want. She wondered if he was aware of that, or if it had been just a careless substitution of words on his part. A careless substitution that had her pulse fluttering like a dizzy butterfly that had completely lost its orientation.

She went with the most logical answer, even though she liked the other better. "The deal was one date. You already went beyond the call."

He looked at her, stunned. "Are you saying no?" That made twice in the space of less than twenty-four hours.

Did he think she was crazy? What unattached woman, living or dead, would turn down a date with him? "I'm saying you don't have to."

He'd *really* never met anyone like her before. "There are things I have to do, Jen," he told her seriously. "I have to make sure I don't do anything that might 'besmirch' the Logan name. I have to make sure not to enter the driver's side of a car after I've had too much to drink, but going out with a woman, in this case you, doesn't come under the heading of 'have to.' This comes under the heading of 'want to.'"

There it was again, that wonderful word. *Want.*

And then it dawned on her. He felt guilty. Guilty because she'd been a virgin and he'd made love with her without knowing that little fact. A warmth filled her heart even though she would have wished he had a different reason for wanting to go out with her.

"Eric, you don't owe me anything because—" Glancing down at Cole, she realized that she couldn't finish the sentence she'd intended, so she merely said euphemistically, "You know."

"I know I don't 'owe' you anything, but maybe I owe me something." He placed his hands on her shoulders. She was a stubborn woman, but then, he rather liked that. Rather liked a great deal about her, he realized. "I'd really like to see you again, Jen." He couldn't put it any plainer than that. "Say yes, Jen," he requested. When she remained silent, looking uncertain, he added, "I'm not accustomed to begging and I'm really not sure I know how."

She wanted to say yes, shout yes, but she was afraid that the moment and the guilt were sweeping him away. She wanted him to ask her after he'd had some time to himself. So she placed her hands on his back, pushing him out across the doorsill.

"Go home and think about it some more," she told him as she eased him out the door.

Well, that certainly had been a first, he thought as he found himself standing on the other side of the closed door. Usually, he had to peel a woman off him after he'd made love with her. Getting another date had never presented a problem before. What was a problem, ordinarily, was maintaining his interest after the initial "chase" was over. His interest, his ardor, usually cooled right after that. This was the first time the chase had begun *after* the first date.

Very interesting, Eric thought as he walked to his car and fished his keys out of his pocket.

"So, what's put that spring in your step?" Rhonda asked as she settled into the desk that was less than five steps away from Jenny's.

Jenny was ordinarily upbeat at work, but this Monday morning she'd set a new high and everyone in the small, crammed office had noticed it.

The attorney who had turned out to be her right arm in this continuous uphill battle was not one who backed off easily. Rhonda Sinclair believed that everything was her business, including the private lives of the people around her.

Jenny wasn't so sure that she wanted to share this time.

Pretending to be deeply engrossed in the reference

material she'd pulled up on her screen, she didn't even look in the older woman's direction. "What?"

Not about to be ignored, Rhonda scooted her chair over until she was beside Jenny's desk. "If you smiled any harder, your face would crack into a million happy little pieces. What gives?" She cocked her head, trying to read the screen. The glare from the window made that impossible. "Find something to make the other side capitulate?"

Jenny knew that Rhonda was referring to the Ortiz case. The matter was still in deliberation, but looked as if it finally might be resolved by the end of the day. She was due in court again early this afternoon. The jury wanted yet something else reread to them, but she had a feeling they were coming to the home stretch.

She grasped at the excuse Rhonda had unwittingly supplied, not wanting to share the small gem she was harboring within her chest. She knew it was silly of her, that Eric wasn't going to call again, no matter what he'd said yesterday. He'd only been paying lip service, saying something that could have been translated to "I'll call you sometime," but it was still early enough for her to be able to pretend that he would.

"I think they just might finally come around today. I don't think they'll be capitulating so much as being felled by the jury's decision." She hadn't had the jury in her pocket, but neither had the opposition, and when push came to shove, a lot of people sided with the little guy. She just had to keep reminding the jury of that every opportunity she had.

Rhonda blew out a breath as she scooted her chair back to her desk. "Nice piece of change for the firm if they do. And none too soon, either." A single woman resigned to remaining that way, Rhonda also doubled as the office manager when Betty was unavailable. It cut down on overhead. "The bill collectors are beginning to congregate in the hall."

Jenny tried to remember if she'd left her checkbook on the counter this morning. She'd written Sandra a check for the week. "I can—"

Rhonda cut her off. "You have. Over and over again." Jenny had been more than generous, underwriting a great many of the firm's expenses, paying them out of her own pocket. "The firm can't run as a Hall charity, especially since you're the only Hall contributing. It's not fair," Rhonda pointed out.

What was money for if you couldn't help people with it? It was an adage that her grandmother had passed on to her and she firmly believed it. "Neither is what some of these people are facing."

Rhonda held up her hands. "Oh, please, you're preaching to the choir, Jenny." The full-figured woman shook her head. "But if you were any more noble, you'd be a plaster statue and I'd be checking you for pigeon droppings."

Jenny pretended to shiver. "Lovely image." She gathered a few papers together, placing them into her briefcase along with her laptop. "Well, I've got to get to court."

Rhonda watched her leave. "Call me the minute you know anything."

Jenny gave her a two-finger salute before she disappeared out the door. "Will do."

He was sitting at the rear of the courtroom.

Her head filled with arguments and statistics, Jenny felt his presence a moment before she actually looked in Eric's direction. Before she saw him.

At first, she thought she wished him there, that he was only a figment of her imagination. But then his eyes met hers and he winked. Her stomach tightened into a huge knot. She knew that her imagination wasn't nearly that powerful.

The judge hadn't entered yet and the hospital's lawyers were talking amongst themselves, looking very confident. She needed a moment to gear up and gather her courage.

Leaning over the last row, she looked at Eric. "What are you doing here?" she whispered.

"I wanted to see you in action again—with your clothes on," he added in a much lower voice, his mouth curving.

She felt color jettisoning itself all through her body, even as a warmth embraced the very core of her.

"Oh, please, not now," she pleaded. She couldn't afford to allow herself to think about making love with Eric now. Her client needed her.

"Sorry." His grin deepened, imprinting itself within her. But he hadn't come to rattle her. "Would you like me to leave?"

It would have been better for her concentration if he didn't stay. But she couldn't bring herself to say that, not when she knew how very finite this all was. From time to time, Jordan would mention the name of a woman Eric was currently seeing. The names were always different. Eric's attention span when it came to women was undoubtedly the shortest measurement of time science had come up with. As far as she was concerned, she'd already outlived her life expectancy when it came to his interest. She didn't want to relinquish a second of what might be left.

"No," she told him, "just don't make any noise."

He nearly laughed. Did she think he was going to try to distract her? "Don't worry, I won't fidget," he promised her.

No, she thought, but she might.

With a nod of her head, she walked up to the front of the court, blocking Eric's presence completely out of her mind.

And becoming Miguel Ortiz's lawyer as well as his last hope.

The jury had asked to hear some more of the testimony reread again. It was the third such request. She glanced over at the hospital's team of lawyers. Each and every one wore a smug look on his or her face. She knew they were confident that they were going to win.

But they were fighting for a corporation and she was fighting for one man who would never walk again. A man who needed the money they were asking for to cover not only his medical bills, but to allow his family to have the kind of life he had been trying to give them by working the three jobs he had. The jobs he no longer could work because of a gross misjudgment on his surgeon's part.

The court stenographer reread the testimony. It took more than twenty minutes. After she had finished, the head of the team of lawyers asked to address the jury again.

Jenny was on her feet, protesting. When she was overruled, she asked for equal time. The judge had no choice but to grant it.

Clenching her fists as she listened, Jenny flashed a reassuring smile at the man sitting beside her in the wheelchair.

"Don't worry," she mouthed to the man.

The moment the other lawyer sat down, Jenny went for the jugular, and for the jury's sympathy. Rising slowly, she crossed to the jury box and made certain she looked at each and every member, making them feel as if she was addressing them exclusively.

"I know this is a hard case, ladies and gentlemen, and you want to get back to your lives. We all do. But Mr. Ortiz has no life to get back to. You see him, barring a miracle, as he will be for the rest of his life. Place yourself in his position. In his chair. Imagine facing the rest of your life in a state of pain, both emotional and physical. Because Mr. Ortiz is a proud man and his pride has been taken away from him.

"Imagine not being able to provide for those you love because of a man who couldn't control his excesses, couldn't think of his patient instead of himself. They tell us that surgeons as skilled as Dr. Turner are a race removed from us. That they have to be because their work requires such deep concentration, is so delicate. Dr. Turner fell from that lofty pedestal—willfully and willingly. By drinking, Dr. Turner turned his scalpel from an instrument of great precision to a blunted knife. And by wielding it, he shattered not just one man's life, but an entire family's.

"This can't be allowed to pass with just a slap on the wrist, with a small fine. Look into your hearts. Think how your loved ones would feel if this was you. Think how you would feel in Mr. Ortiz's place. And please, come back with what you believe to be a fair judgment."

She sat back down, praying.

The jury filed out for what she hoped was the final time.

Finally, all the waiting was over. Holding her client's hand to give him moral support, Jenny held her breath as the judge and the jury foreman went through the proper motions of questions and answers.

"We find for the plaintiff in the sum of ten million dollars."

Jenny's mouth dropped open. The amount was twice what they had asked for.

The next few minutes were a blur. She remembered looking over toward the other table, remembered thinking that she had never seen six such solemn people. But there were no cries of an appeal, no veiled warnings. In their hearts, the lawyers knew the judgment was fair and that contesting it would only be courting more bad publicity. The hospital would have enough trouble recovering from this.

Dayley, the head of the team, curtly told her that checks would be cut by the end of the week. And then he and the others filed out even as Miguel Ortiz's family and friends all converged around them, whooping their approval. She was vaguely aware that the judge had withdrawn. And acutely aware that Eric was still in the back of the courtroom.

He liked the way joy radiated from every part of her as he watched her hug the man in the wheelchair.

Miguel kissed both of her hands, thanking her in two languages.

"You are my new patron saint," Miguel told her. "We must celebrate. You come to my house, bring your family, your parents, everyone." His invitation was echoed by his wife and children. "We will have a huge fiesta."

Jenny thought of her family. Without realizing that they were prejudiced, her parents regarded people such as Miguel and his family as "the help." They would be as out of place at Miguel's celebration as a Rembrandt in a room full of Picassos.

"I'm afraid my family won't be able to make it. But I do have a little boy," she told him.

"Bring him." Miguel's dark eyes shifted to Eric who was approaching them. "And bring your young man, too."

Jenny stiffened, expecting to see Eric protest and then bolt. "Oh, no, he's not—"

But to her surprise, Eric didn't retreat. Instead, he slipped his arm around her waist.

"I'd love to come. Name the time and the place." The smile he wore as he looked at her went straight to her gut like a torpedo. "Looks like I get that second date after all."

Fourteen

It astounded Jennifer just how well Eric fit in.

Oh, he still stood out, but that was because he was so good-looking, not because his manner created an imaginary circle around him, setting him apart from the other men and women attending Miguel Ortiz's celebration that following Saturday.

He'd surprised her by showing up to escort her and Cole to the party. She'd thought he was only paying lip service when he said he would come, but he'd arrived a full half hour early, wearing clothes far more casual than she'd ever seen on him. His jeans were worn and adhered to his body like a second skin. She caught herself staring a lot and suppressing sighs.

He'd further surprised her by speaking flawless, fluent Spanish to some of the children, who at first were shy with him before they finally ventured out.

"I thought you didn't speak Spanish," she reminded him, thinking of what he'd said when Miguel had referred to him as *"su novio."*

He'd grinned at her and winked. "Sometimes it's useful to play dumb."

He wasn't playing dumb now. As Jenny watched in complete awe, Eric played not only with Cole, but with the other children who were attending the party. He got along so well with them that Miguel's wife asked him to take charge of the piñata that was hung out in the small backyard.

Herding the children before him, with some of the parents following, Eric organized them in order of size so that the little ones had first crack at the festively decorated cardboard donkey that held several pounds of candy and prizes in its belly.

To Jenny's everlasting gratitude, he even managed to coax Cole into joining in.

Because he was so small for his age, Cole wound up being the second one up. He stood eyeing the donkey for several minutes before Eric placed the long, slender stick in his hands. He allowed him a practice swing, even guiding his arms, before he finally slipped the blindfold over his eyes and gently spun him around.

Cole, like his predecessor, swung three times and missed making contact each time. As he slipped off the blindfold, Eric was filled with nothing but praise for the boy's efforts, erasing any dejection that failure might have left in its wake.

He ruffled the boy's hair as Cole made room for the next contender. "Great job, Cole. You practice that swing and the Mariners are going to want you for their lineup in another sixteen years."

The number stuck in her head, as did the smile that bloomed on Cole's face in response. In sixteen more years, Cole would be twenty, a good age for a rookie. Eric had remembered how old her son was.

Her heart swelled.

That was the moment, she realized, the moment she actually fell in love with Eric. Really in love. This wasn't a wild, passionate sensation that was some outgrowth of a girlhood fantasy, and it wasn't because he'd completely stopped her world last Saturday by making love with her. She felt the way she did because Eric Logan was good and kind and decent.

And because he'd touched her son, not just saving his life, but coaxing out his soul.

She wrapped her arms around herself as she continued watching Eric and her son. He was feeding the boy a quesadilla and she could swear she heard Cole's chuckling. If life could be any more perfect, she didn't think that she could stand it.

"He didn't wake up the whole trip home," Eric commented, looking into the back seat where the boy sat. Cole was strapped into the car seat Eric had transferred from Jenny's car, the boy's head listing to one side. He was completely and soundly asleep.

"He had a big day." They both had, she added silently. "I haven't seen him play like that since before Rachel died." She looked at Eric as he drew the boy slowly out of the car seat. Her heart swelled again. She swore that man was going to make her heart break apart. "Thank you."

He shut the door with his back and, carrying the boy, began walking very slowly toward her apartment. "For what? You're the one who invited me, I should thank you."

"Miguel invited you," she pointed out. "I wouldn't have had the nerve."

He stopped at the edge of the first step leading up to her place. They'd made love a week ago, how could she be shy around him?

"Why not?"

Turning away from him, she fished out her house key and opened the door. "Because I didn't think that you'd want to go to something like that."

"Why not?" The apartment felt chilly after the heated car. Slanting a glance in her direction, he smiled to himself, thinking of the way he wanted to turn the heat up in here. "It was fun."

She flipped on the light switch before leading the way to Cole's room. She couldn't help thinking how natural Eric looked, holding the boy that way.

"I know." She'd had a wonderful time herself,

once she'd relaxed about his being there. The first ten minutes after she'd arrived had been spent in fear that Eric might say something to offend someone. "But, well, people in the world you come from only see people like Miguel's family as gardeners and busboys and—"

He waited for her to pull back the covers, then laid the boy down on the bed. "Am I really that bad?"

Jenny couldn't tell if she'd made him angry or not, but it was too late to backtrack. There was no such thing as un-uttering a sentence.

"No, you're not," she was quick to assure him, then admitted, "I guess I was just thinking of my parents." She didn't want him getting the wrong idea. Her parents were good people in their own way, just isolated despite their boatload of friends. "It's not that they mean to be cruel or condescending, it's just the way things have always been and, well..." Her voice trailed off. She was making it worse by talking. Jenny shifted courses. "I didn't know you spoke Spanish."

Eric knew what she was doing, but there was no graceful way out of this, so he let her slide.

"There are a lot of things about me you don't know." He felt the attraction that had been simmering all day growing, taking on proportions that couldn't easily be controlled. "A lot of things about you that I don't know. But I'd like to learn."

And he meant that. It surprised him, but he did. He wanted to know her favorite color, and what she'd watched as a kid. What made her laugh. What made her sad. And he wanted to know about the entire spectrum in between.

He nodded toward the sleeping boy on the bed. "What do you say we get this little guy settled and the learning can begin?"

Excitement pricked against her skin, making all the soft little hairs at the back of her neck stand up on end. Because they were suddenly so dry, she unconsciously wet her lips. And saw Eric looking at her mouth. The excitement heightened.

"Sounds like a good plan to me."

They tucked Cole into bed together. The boy slept through the entire process of having his shoes and socks removed, his jeans and sweatshirt exchanged for a pair of pajamas. The only resistance he offered was a tiny moan, but his eyes never opened.

Eric looked down at the pattern woven all through Cole's fresh pajamas. "Batman?"

She smiled fondly at the boy, lightly brushing his hair away from his face. He looked so serene, so untroubled. She wished he was like that when he was awake. *Soon,* she promised herself. *Soon.*

"His favorite," she told Eric.

"Mine, too." She looked at him in surprise and he laughed. "I drove my mother crazy asking for my own utility belt. She finally had someone create one for me. The pockets inside the belt were all filled with jelly beans and hard candy." That summer he had become something more than a walking stick.

He had had girth and mass, which he began to mold the following fall by religiously adhering to a work-out video when no one else was looking. "I thought that was pretty cool, too."

She could almost see him in it, rushing around the house in a mask and cape, promising to revenge him-self on evil as he popped candy into his mouth. She shook her head.

"You must have been one hell of a little boy."

"They say the boy is the father of the man." He slipped his arms around her, drawing her to him in the short hallway between her bedroom and Cole's. "What do you think?"

It was as if the very air had opted to stand still again. It certainly wasn't moving around with any noticeable speed or direction. She dragged a breath into her lungs. "I think that if you don't kiss me right now, I'm going to explode."

He cupped her cheek, thinking how soft she felt. And how incredibly tempting. "I was just thinking the same thing. Funny how great minds work alike."

"Funny," she murmured in agreement, wrapping her arms around his neck.

Wrapping herself around him.

There was no preheat setting, no momentary lag before the passion caught up to them. It was right there, waiting to take over.

To take them prisoner.

He kissed her over and over again, each time

deeper, each time hungrier than the last. Eric slid his hands over her body with the certainty of someone who knew what was his and was still in awe of it.

In a tangle of bodies, kisses and swiftly mushrooming desires, they found their way into her bedroom, closing the door before either one of them had the presence of mind or the strength to pay further attention to any extraneous matters.

Within a heartbeat, he'd stripped her of her sweater and her bra. He could feel the blood pounding in his veins, urging him on. Eric filled his hands with her breasts then brought his lips to them, sampling the sweet, tangy taste of her skin.

His heart slamming against his ribs like a deranged prisoner trying to break through his restraining iron bars, Eric stepped back, shedding his own pullover and tossing it to the floor. As he moved toward her, she surprised him by undoing his belt and then opening the snap at his jeans. Her fingertips lightly scraped against his belly.

The part of him that didn't feel as if a blowtorch was being passed over it was almost amused by her boldness. Amused by the contrast from the woman he'd thought she was to the woman she'd turned out to be.

Or maybe, just maybe, Jenny was this way because of him.

It was a vain thought, but he liked it, liked that she was this way just with him and no one else. Heaven help him, he liked the fact that he was her first. That she was his exclusively.

The thought all but rattled his world. He had never, ever, wanted anyone to be his exclusively. Because exclusivity brought with it a silent promise, a responsibility he wanted no part of.

And here he was, liking it.

Wanting it.

Wanting her.

Passion exploded in his veins and he held her hands, guiding them as she tugged the zipper down, then pulled the jeans from his thighs.

Her eyes met his. He saw a glimmer of amusement in them. "Not doing it right?" she breathed.

His grin was lopsided and went straight to her heart. "Not doing it fast enough," he countered.

The next moment, he was working her jeans off. Her underwear was all but yanked away in his urgency to have all of her standing before him the way she had first been created.

Because there was a fire in his veins, he sought to spread it, sought to draw her into the burning ring.

Eric kissed her over and over again, reducing her into loud, raspy breaths, into twisting desire. She couldn't get enough of him, feel enough of him.

More. The word kept echoing in her brain like an endless refrain. More.

And even more wasn't enough.

This was incredible, Jenny thought. He was raising her to heights she hadn't known could be achieved. Last time she would have sworn with certainty that she'd felt it all, experienced all there was to experience. But she was wrong. Happily wrong. Now he was doing things, such wondrous, delicious things, to her body, to her very being. Every inch of her wracked with explosions as he brought her from climax to climax, using his hands, his lips, his tongue.

He was very nearly driving her insane. But it was a wonderful way to leave this earth.

She gasped as the latest of an innumerable collection began to recede, her body as slick from all this as his. It took her a moment to focus on his face, another moment to force the words out of her throat. "So…tell me…have…there been…many…deaths…from…pleasure?"

Eric laughed. She was tiring him out, but he wasn't complaining. "None that I know of." Summoning the last bit of strength he had, Eric raised himself up, sliding his body along hers until he was over her. He looked deeply into her eyes, loving them more each time he did so. "Why, are you in danger of that?"

"Yes." The word was hardly an audible sigh. He had to lean in closely to hear her.

He grinned. "Me, too."

Lacing his hands through hers, Eric slowly drove himself into her. He watched the passion flourish in her eyes. Echo in his soul. Stir him in ways he'd never known he could be stirred.

She was his and he was hers and it was good.

Slowly he began the rhythm that they both craved, knowing that it wouldn't be the last time. Not even for tonight.

She found herself humming songs whose titles she couldn't remember. It didn't matter, she hummed them anyway. Just as her soul was humming.

Two weeks and there was no sign of an end.

Two weeks and Eric had been a part of almost every day, every evening.

Every night.

He'd shown up in her office and made Rhonda visibly drool. The older woman made no bones about the fact that she now envied her on more than just a professional level. Jenny found it incredible.

Whenever he could get away, Eric was there in court, to silently cheer her on, or at the law library when she was doing research.

Moreover, he'd shown up on her doorstep, with picnic dinners, with tickets for movies, with videos of old TV programs he loved and she had never heard of. With Christmas decorations for the tree she and Cole were decorating. She'd been triumphant because she'd gotten Cole to help. Having Eric there, as well, made the experience indescribable.

Eric made a point of including Cole in everything that involved her outside of work.

The little boy was blossoming beneath the attention. He responded to Eric in a way that brought tears to her eyes and made her heart sing. It got to the point that she knew Cole was looking forward to Eric's next visit. Just as she was.

And the nights… The nights were wondrous, sparkling slices of heaven. She tried not to get carried away, tried not to get spoiled. Each time he stayed, she told herself it would be the last time, that he would lose interest in her and that she should just be happy with what she'd had. But she knew in her heart that she wanted it to go on, against all odds and common sense.

She did her best to make the evenings memorable for both of them.

And the next evening, as she held her breath and crossed her fingers, he returned and she fell in love with him a little more.

Even with an end she knew was coming, an end that was looming somewhere in the shadows, Jenny still couldn't remember ever being happier.

It was one of those days that made her feel like a trailer park beset by not just one tornado, but three. She no sooner defused one crisis than another one popped up. She found herself manning phones because Rhonda was in court and their communal secretary, Betty, was down with her umpteenth cold. One of their other lawyers, Jack, was out of town, gathering evidence. Or so she vaguely remembered hearing him tell her. And Foster, the fourth lawyer on their tiny team, had decided that he was taking a vacation.

She felt besieged and beleaguered, but finally, by noon, a pocket of quiet descended on her. She felt like putting her head down on the desk and catching a quick nap, but knew she'd be flirting with disaster if she did. She'd never been one of those people to wake up refreshed from a nap. Rather she'd always felt as if a lobotomy had been performed on her while she'd had her eyes closed.

But at least she could enjoy the quiet for however long it lasted. Maybe she could even manage to get some of her own work done rather than carting it home.

Eric hadn't popped up today, but she reminded herself that the man did have a life and a position to maintain. If she was lucky, she'd see him tonight. The thought kept her going.

A short, staccato noise alerted her that the door was being opened. Someone else had found his way into their legal aid office. She tried to put on her best face.

It melted away, to be replaced by a genuine smile when she saw her brother walking toward her.

"Oh, thank God."

"Many women say that when they see me," Jordan cracked as he deposited himself into the chair beside her desk.

She dragged her hand through her hair, trying to center herself. It took less than a minute. She'd been so happy lately, no amount of strife could separate her from her buoyancy for long.

Unable to work in chaos, Jenny started putting away the files she'd pulled out earlier. "So, to what do I owe this honor?"

"I was in the neighborhood and thought I'd take my favorite sister to lunch." He leaned back in the chair, watching her as she moved around the small office. "You look like your feet are barely touching the ground." He laced his hands together behind his head. "Anything I should know about?"

She paused to look at her brother. "You mean he hasn't told you?"

"He?"

She gave him a reproving look. As if he didn't know. "Eric."

Jordan smiled. "Why don't you tell me?"

Maybe he truly didn't know, Jenny thought. She didn't stop to analyze why. "I guess you could say we're seeing each other."

His grin threatened to split his face. "You're glowing."

There was no reason to deny it. "I guess I am." She resumed putting the files back in their drawers, then stopped. There was more to that grin on her brother's face than met the eye. "What are you looking so smug about?"

"Nothing."

He never could pull off innocence. She crossed back to him, still holding the last file. Something uncertain fluttered through her, but she banked it down. She had a habit of overthinking things, she told herself. "Jordan, I know that look. What do you know?"

He shrugged. "That I did a good thing."

She cocked her head, studying him. "You mean twisting Eric's arm to go to the auction?"

He held his hands up. "There was very little twisting involved. I'm just glad I talked Lola into it."

The smile on Jenny's face slowly melted away. "Into what?"

When he said nothing, Jenny pressed again, an ominous feeling growing in the pit of her stomach, warning her away. But she couldn't just let this drop. She wasn't one to run from things.

"Into what?" she asked again and looked down at him squarely. "Jordan, what did you do? Tell me the truth."

Jordan sighed. "I asked her to bid on Eric for you."

She felt as if her head had suddenly been submerged in an icy cold lake.

"You asked her. To bid on Eric. For me." The words left her lips slowly like small foreign entities that didn't understand one another. And then the horror, the embarrassment, began to make itself known to her. "How could you?"

"Jenny, you've always liked him. I know you did."

How could he? How *could* he? The question kept echoing in her head. She stared at him in disbelief, feeling naked and violated. "So you did what, got your poor, plain sister a pity date?"

"It's not like that. I thought you'd be happy."

"I was. I would have been—under the right circumstances."

Words were eluding her, burning up in the face of her shame. Had Eric been laughing at her the whole time? She couldn't believe it, didn't want to believe it, but what else could it have been? He was so popular and she was just Jordan's little sister.

Under attack, Jordan tried to defend himself. "You thought a bunch of friends got together to give you a dream date. How is this so different?"

How could he even ask that? What had Eric been thinking the entire time they'd been together? And Cole, how was Cole going to react to all this? He'd actually been getting close to Eric.

She felt an ache growing in her chest. "Because you're my brother. Because you're his friend." She drew herself up, furious. This was something her mother was capable of, but Jordan… She thought Jordan knew better. She'd thought he was on her side. "Did you have to pay him to go out with me?"

"Of course not." Then, no doubt realizing he was shouting, he lowered his voice. "Eric doesn't even know I was behind this."

Eric and Jordan were friends, close friends. She knew they shared a great deal. That her brother wouldn't tell Eric what he was up to seemed impossible to her.

"I don't believe you." Jenny squared her shoulders. There was nowhere to go to escape the hurt. She felt tears building. "You might as well go, Jordan. I won't be having lunch today. I suddenly lost my appetite."

"Jenny—" He placed his hand on her shoulder, but she shrugged him off.

"Just go, okay?"

When he did, when she saw that she was alone, she laid her head down on the desk and cried as she felt her heart breaking into a million tiny pieces.

Fifteen

"Hi."

Startled, she swung around to see Eric standing inside the office. Ever since she'd sent Jordan away less than fifteen minutes ago, she'd been so lost in her own thoughts, in her own pain, trying to regain control over herself before Rhonda returned, she hadn't even heard the door opening.

This time, when her heart thudded against her chest, it felt leaden.

All this time she'd been pretending, secretly hoping.... God, what a fool she'd been, what an A-number-one fool.

Eric saw the strange expression on her face. Was something wrong? he thought.

"I've never seen it so empty in here before." He looked around at the cluttered desks. Usually, the place was overflowing with people. He decided to keep it light until she told him what was going on. "Have you championed all the causes there were to champion?"

As early as this morning, she would have taken that to be a teasing remark. Now she knew better. He was laughing at her. Why else would someone like Eric Logan, who could have any dynamic, well connected, easy woman he wanted, be spending time with her?

For laughs. Or pity. She wasn't sure which one was worse.

Jenny struggled to keep emotion out of her voice, but she could feel it welling up in her throat. "We're in between appointments for once. Rhonda's in court, Jack's out of state, Foster's on vacation and Betty's out sick."

He crossed to her, reaching for her waist. She pulled away. Why? "Well, you look healthy enough. Not that your having a cold would keep me away."

With the file cabinet drawer between them, she looked at him. *Was I entertaining enough for you? Have you told your friends about Jordan's sister yet? What a little idiot she is, thinking there was something going on between the two of you?* "What would keep you away?"

Now he *really* knew something was wrong. She wasn't the woman whose bed he'd left in the wee hours of this morning. This was a different, colder person. "What?"

"What's your time limit on this—this joke…this project…" She waved her hands about impotently. "Whatever you call it."

Was he missing something here? "I'm not following you."

She wouldn't be turning around to see him at the back of the courtroom, or walking up to her through the stacks of the law library, or popping up on her doorstep. And he wouldn't be there for Christmas, she suddenly thought. She wouldn't have him to look forward to anymore. Well, she'd survived other things, she'd survive this, too. "No, I don't suppose you will be for much longer."

Trying to make sense out of what she was saying to him, Eric failed. He frowned. "Jen, I'm not fluent in gibberish. What are you saying?"

How long did he intend to pretend to be innocent? Dumb didn't become him.

"That you've put in your time. More than your time." She saw confusion crease his brow. Maybe the man should have been an actor. "It's okay. You've done your bit for charity." She hardened her jaw. Mostly to keep it from trembling. "More than your bit. You can go back to your life now."

He blew out a breath. This was getting worse, not better. And for some reason, she was obviously angry at him for something. "Well, you've gone from gibberish to babbling. Any chance English is going to slip in any time soon?"

"You want English?" She slammed the file cabinet drawer shut and took the two steps that had her going toe-to-toe with him. What she lacked in stature she made up in anger. "I'll give you English. I am *not* a charity case. I might seem like one to someone like you, but I'm not. I have my pride, damn it. Maybe you think you're doing me some kind of 'service,' but you're not. You don't have to waste any more of your precious time and your considerable charm on me."

His mouth dropped open. *Nice touch,* she thought sarcastically. The man *was* a born actor.

"And don't worry, I'm not about to sit by my window, waiting for some prince to climb up my trellis, reciting poetry." God, when she thought of what a fool she must have seemed like, all she wanted to do was cry. Or punch him. "I'm a big girl now and I know those kind of things only happen in fairy tales." She raised herself up on her toes, her eyes nearly level with his. "And I don't believe in fairy tales."

For a second, he felt a flare of temper. He had no idea what she thought he'd done to merit this outburst. "Do you believe in therapy? Because I think you might need a little. Maybe a lot," he amended. He looked at the cases that were piled high on her desk. "This job has gotten to you."

She placed herself in front of the files and directly in his line of vision. "No, it hasn't. My job is the only thing that keeps me sane. Sort of," she felt obligated to tack on.

Eric tried to find alternate reasons, although it

was reaching. The Jenny he knew wasn't given to these kinds of excesses. "Then did someone slip something into your coffee? Have you been smoking something? Because you're just not making any sense."

How long was he going to go on with this charade? Jenny asked herself. She didn't have time for this, so she ended it. "I *know,* Eric. I know."

He blew out a breath. "Well, that makes one of us. Care to share with the class?"

How could he be making jokes? But then, this whole thing was probably one big joke to him, wasn't it? *She* was one big joke to him. "I know my brother put the money up for the bid."

"Bid? What bid?"

Okay, if he was going to play dumb, she'd spell it out for him. "At the auction. For the bid on you." When he still looked confused, her patience began to shatter. "My brother had Lola Wilcox bid on you for me."

She still wasn't making any sense, but Eric was trying to unravel her words. His eyebrows drew together over the bridge of his nose. "You wanted to go out with me?"

"Yes— No, damn it." Eric was trying to confuse the issue, confuse her. And she wasn't about to let him. "Jordan didn't tell me he was doing it. I thought… I thought…"

Her voice trailed off weakly. Just how much better did it sound that she thought her friends had gotten together to bid on him in order to give her a night she would never forget?

Jordan was right, she thought, it sounded equally as bad. It just felt worse to know that her brother had orchestrated this, that was all.

At least part of this was becoming a little less obscure. Eric sat on the corner of her desk. "Well, he didn't tell me, either. All he did was ask me to volunteer when you asked—" He stopped, letting the kernel of information, such as it was, sink in. "So Jordan cooked all this up, did he?"

Hands on her hips—to keep from slugging him—Jenny glared at him. "Don't look so damn amused."

Eric raised his hands in innocent surrender. He was trying not to laugh at the fierce expression on Jenny's face. She looked adorable when she was angry, but he didn't think she'd appreciate hearing that right now. "I'm just surprised, that's all."

Surprised that his best friend was so intuitive when he hadn't seen what was there, right before his eyes. That Jenny was a fiery woman who just needed the right set of circumstances to bring her inner fire out of her. And he'd been lucky enough to be instrumental in that.

She was magnificent, he thought as she continued to dress him down. This was the passion he'd seen in the courtroom, the passion he'd experienced first-hand when they made love. There was no doubt about it, Jenny was utterly different from the woman he'd thought she was, the woman she appeared to be to the unobservant eye.

In the short time since the auction, he'd had an intensified course in Jennifer Hall. And he liked what he'd learned. She didn't rest on her family's laurels and money. Instead, she chose to go her own way and to take on causes for the poor and underprivileged. She believed in all the fights she undertook, believed in fighting for the underdog. He found that both admirable and inspiring. There was no doubt in his mind that they connected on so many levels.

And he intended to have them continue connecting. But to do that, he was going to have to set her straight about a few things. And get her to stop shouting at him.

He thought of kissing her. That would bring about an immediate silence, but he was afraid she might take it as an insult, so he tried to break through her rhetoric. It wasn't easy. She was, after all, a lawyer.

Finally, when she stopped for a breath, he managed to get in more than half a word. He tried to make the most of it. "Listen, Jenny, I don't know what you think happened, but—"

Oh, no, he wasn't going to blind her with his charm. She already knew she wasn't immune to it. Summoning all the inner strength she had available, she said the same thing to him that she'd said to Jordan, but with more feeling because she could feel her heart bleeding inside her.

How stupid of her to think that they could have a

chance, that Eric could have feelings for her that were even a quarter of what she was feeling for him.

"Go, just go."

Eric tried to put his hands on her shoulders. Maybe he thought he was somehow harnessing the anger within her, but she shrugged him off. She couldn't think when he touched her. All she wanted to do was melt against him. But she was through melting, through being the pathetic, lovesick puppy. She knew he was trying to apologize. In his own way, he probably hadn't meant to hurt her. After all, this had all started out because of a charity event.

Well, she didn't need his charity.

She backed away from him before he could reach for her again. "I said *go.*"

He debated taking hold of her, making her listen to reason, but decided that she needed a little time to cool off.

And he needed time to think this through himself. The next step he took might just seal his fate and he wanted to make sure that he wanted to take it.

"Okay," he said, retreating to the front door. "Have it your way. I'm going."

Fight for me, damn it, a small voice pleaded as she saw the door close.

Stupid right up to the end, aren't you? she mocked herself as she turned away.

Because Rhonda returned to the office ten minutes later, followed shortly by not one new client but three, Jenny forced herself to focus and act as if there was nothing wrong. Like someone hadn't just driven a Mack truck right through her life.

She managed to hold it together until she came home. Until after Sandra, who looked at her as if she sensed something was wrong, had finally ceased asking probing questions and gone home for the night.

It was only then that she allowed herself to collapse onto the sofa, to curl up like a lost, hurt child, to rest her face against her knees and sob.

She sobbed so hard she wasn't sure if she could ever stop.

She didn't know how long she sat there, crying, telling herself to stop, telling herself she had to suck it up and take care of the little boy who was in his room. Five minutes, ten, half an hour, she didn't know. Everything had stopped around her.

And then she felt a little hand on her shoulder and heard a small voice saying, "Don't cry, Mommy, don't cry. It's gonna be okay."

Mommy.

Her eyes, glistening with tears, widened as she raised her head from her knees and looked at the boy. "What did you just call me?" she asked hoarsely, trying desperately to clear her throat.

Cole didn't answer immediately. Instead, he continued patting her shoulder and then he repeated, "Don't cry, Mommy."

The tears flowed harder, but this time, they were tears of joy.

Close a door, open a window. Wasn't that something she'd heard once? So she'd lost Eric, her *dream* of Eric, she amended, but she'd gotten a huge breakthrough with Cole and that was what truly mattered.

Cole. Her Cole.

He'd called her Mommy.

She held the boy to her, hugging him for all she was worth. Grateful for the small miracle. "Oh, God, I love you, Cole."

"You're squishing me," he finally protested, his voice muffled, his breath hot against her chest.

Drawing him back, Jenny laughed through her tears. Very gently, she combed her fingers through his hair. "Sorry." She kissed his forehead lightly. "It won't happen again."

She had a great deal to be grateful for, she reminded herself. She was in the right place to help people who desperately needed someone in their corner to fight their battles for them, and she had Cole, who meant the world to her. So many people had so much less.

Drying her eyes with the back of her hand, Jenny drew the little boy onto her lap. Already she could feel the sun trying to break through inside of her. "What say you and I go out for some ice cream?"

He wiggled around in her lap to look at her. "Eric, too?"

Oh, honey, this is going to hurt you, too, isn't it? She tried to sound as cheerful as she could. "No, not Eric, too."

Cole cocked his head, his green eyes intent on hers. "Why?"

She tried to take the easy way out. After all, children liked simplicity, right? "Because he's not here right now."

Cole scrambled off her lap and then went to the cordless telephone. He brought the receiver back with him and presented it to her. "Call him."

Yes, this was simple, too, she thought. She wished she could be a child again, when life wasn't complicated.

She searched for a plausible explanation that would satisfy the boy. She had only herself to blame for the uphill battle before her, that of getting Cole to forget about Eric.

"I'm afraid—"

Jenny stopped, listening. Was that music? She could have sworn that the strains of a mariachi band, like the one she'd heard at Miguel's house, were drifting into the apartment despite the fact that all the windows were closed.

"Music," Cole told her, pointing toward the sliding glass doors.

"You hear it, too, huh?" It did sound as if it was coming from the rear of the development. Curious, she crossed to the patio door that led out onto her tiny balcony. The balcony overlooked a rather steep drop at the rear of the complex, in the center of which was a man-made pond. The small, bubbling ponds were standard issue for all the apartments and had been what had sold her on renting here in the first place.

Opening the door, she saw that there were three people dressed in mariachi regalia, standing next to the pond, playing *Maria Elena,* the song she'd liked so much at Miguel Ortiz's party. Looking closer, she realized that the three people playing were Miguel's brother, his son and daughter.

Miguel's brother, Santos, waved at her with his maracas and indicated the trellis that ran along the length of the apartment building, over two stories.

Her mouth fell open.

Eric was on the trellis, slowly making his way up to her window. The trellis creaked and issued warnings with each movement.

"'How do I love thee, let me count the ways…'" he began, raising his voice to be heard above the music.

"Are you out of your mind?" she demanded, thunderstruck.

He stopped, mentally bookmarking the poem so he could resume reciting it. "You said something about sitting by your window, waiting for a prince to climb up a trellis while reciting poetry," he reminded her.

He *was* out of his mind, she thought. But something within her was stirred anyway. This wasn't part of laughing at her. If anything, this was part of a death wish.

"I said I *wasn't* going to sit by my— Oh, never

mind. You're going to break your neck," she all but shrieked at him. "You climb down off that thing right now," she insisted.

Eric held firm, wondering how much time he had before the trellis decided to give way. It really didn't feel very stable. He hoped she wouldn't take long making up her mind. "I can't climb down, not until you tell me you forgive me—although technically I didn't do anything."

She could feel panic welling up within her. "I—"

He thought he'd move her along a little. He didn't relish the thought of getting bruised. "Better talk fast, this thing feels like it's going to give."

She thought she saw a portion of the trellis begin to separate from the wall and list. "Okay, okay, I forgive you. You didn't do anything wrong. It was Jordan's fault—"

"Why?" he wanted to know. "For getting us together? I don't know about you, but I'm kind of grateful to him for that."

"Yeah, right." He was going to fall, she just knew it. "Eric, please come in."

Jenny reached for him, but he put his hand up to block her, then quickly grabbed hold of the trellis again. "Okay, but under one condition—"

She could feel the air backing up in her lungs as she watched the trellis. Praying. "I already said I forgive you."

"Now say you'll marry me."

Her mouth dropped open again. "What?" He *had* to be kidding this time. Why was he doing this to her? "Eric, it's not April first yet."

"I know that. And the only fool here'll be me if I lose the only woman worth loving in this world."

Did he think he was being kind? Didn't he realize how much he was hurting her with this? "You don't have to say those things."

How did he make her understand? Why was she so convinced he wasn't serious?

"Don't you get it yet? I *want* to say those things." His eyes were on hers. "I look into your eyes and I'm home. I've never felt like this before, Jen. I don't want to lose that. Ever." He almost gave in to the temptation of climbing onto her balcony, but he knew he had to hold out, had to get her to agree first. He gave it his best shot. "I might not have said it yet, but I love you."

Her whole soul felt as if it was melting, "No, you haven't said it yet," she whispered, numbly staring at him. "You love me?"

"I wouldn't risk life and limb if I didn't." Just then, the trellis gave a mighty groan.

She reached for him again, feeling panic building. He was going to kill himself if he didn't climb in. "Eric, please come in—"

But he hung there, shaking his head to her plea. "Not until you say yes."

"Yes!" She shouted the word at him. She would have shouted any word he wanted just to get him inside and on firm territory again.

He saw through her. "Say 'yes' that you'll marry me."

He was being impetuous, she just knew it. Once he was thinking clearly again, he'd rescind the proposal. And there was Cole to think about.

"Eric, please think about this." She slipped her arm around the small boy who had nuzzled his way forward, trying to see what was happening. "It's a package deal."

His eyes just level with the balcony, Eric smiled at the boy. Cole grinned back. "I'm counting on it."

Cole looked up at her. There was an eagerness in his eyes she hadn't seen all these long months. "Am I gonna have a daddy, too?"

Eric turned his eyes on her, as well. "It's up to Mommy, cowboy."

Cole looked at her hopefully. "Please, Mommy?"

"Yes, please Mommy," Eric echoed. The trellis groaned more ominously.

"Yes, yes, yes," she cried.

Leaning forward, Jenny made a grab for Eric's arm just as the trellis gave every indication it was going to start separating from the building. Holding on to Eric with both hands, she finally managed to pull him in. Cole grabbed on to his arm as he came over the balcony, and all three tumbled to the floor in a heap.

Her heart was still racing as she anticlimactically declared, "I've got you!"

Eric was on his knees before her, and pulled her

up to hers. “Yes,” he told her, framing her face. “You do.”

Standing up beside them, Cole wrapped his small arms about his new mommy and daddy and cried, “Yippee” just as the latter kissed the former.

* * * * *

Turn the page for a sneak preview
of the next emotional LOGAN'S LEGACY *title,*
A PRECIOUS GIFT
by USA TODAY *bestselling author*
Karen Rose Smith
on sale in November 2004...

One

Carrie Summers paced the blue-and-white tiled general reception area in the Children's Connection Adoption Center. Her husband was fifteen minutes late, and she was afraid that meant Brian had changed his mind about adopting. They'd answered question after question and submitted to a home study that was now finished. This was their last meeting with the caseworker before they were put into the system.

Brian was never late.

He was a man of his word—a man she'd always been able to depend upon. But for the past three years of their five-year marriage, tension had built between them. When they'd married, Carrie had been so in love, so absolutely sure their wedding vows would be everlasting. However, she had a secret, and the repercussions of that secret were pushing them apart.

If only Brian could embrace the idea of an adoption wholeheartedly. If only Brian could accept an adopted child as his own.

"Are you ready?" a deep, male voice asked.

She'd been watching the double glass doors leading outside to the unusually sunny January day. Rain always fell on Portland, Oregon, this time of year. Now she swung around and faced the man whose voice always vibrated through her like a heartfelt song.

"Where did you come from?" she asked with a smile, trying to hide her anxiety over his lateness.

"There was something I had to do before this meeting."

Brian Summers was six foot two, muscular, incredibly fit and more handsome than any man Carrie had ever seen. His thick tawny hair waved over his brow, and he kept it in a clipped short style to suit his image—the image of a real estate developer on the go, a millionaire who cared less about his appearance than the powerhouse deals he brokered. When they'd first met she'd known that he'd spoken to her at that cocktail party because she'd looked like the model she'd been. Although her black dress had been demure and classic, his eyes had lingered often on her dark red hair and the angles of her face, as well as her figure. Their attraction had been mutual, and that night she'd hoped Brian could see beyond her outward appearance. He'd seemed to, and that's why she'd fallen in love with him.

"You've had a meeting in the hospital?" Land development deals didn't usually begin at Portland General.

"No, nothing like that."

Just then, the door to the reception area from the inner offices opened and a middle-aged brunette smiled at them. "Are you Carrie and Brian Summers?"

They answered in unison. "Yes."

"You'll be meeting with me today." She extended her hand first to Brian and then to Carrie. "I'm Trina Bentley."

"We've gone through this whole process with Stacy Williams," Brian said with a frown.

"Yes, I know you have. Stacy's out with the flu. Since this last meeting is simply a formality, I told her I'd take it for her so we can give you the official okay and find you a baby. Come on back to my office."

In their first years together, Brian had always been solicitous of Carrie, often showing affection by a touch of his hand on her shoulder, his arm around her waist. They hadn't touched as much recently, not since the in vitro attempts had failed. Now as they walked side by side, the sleeve of Brian's suit jacket brushed her arm. She felt the jolt of his close proximity through the sleeve of her cream wool dress.

Everything about the Children's Connection Adoption Center was bright and welcoming, including Trina's office. It was pale yellow with a bulletin board on the wall covered with pictures of children, from infants to teenagers.

The caseworker motioned to the two upholstered chairs in front of her desk. "Have a seat. I promise I'll make this as painless as possible."

Carrie stole a glance at Brian. He hadn't liked discussing the details of his life with a stranger. He was a private man, and he hadn't appreciated answering questions about his work habits, family history and finances. The poking and prodding into his personal and business life had rankled. Yet today he seemed calmer…more accepting about the whole thing, and Carrie wondered why.

Opening the folder on her desk, Trina glanced over the pages as if she were familiar with them. "I've read through everything including the home-study report." Leaning back in her chair, she focused her hazel eyes on Carrie. "You've been through a lot."

Panicking, Carrie's mouth went dry. Could this woman somehow know…?

Trina went on, "You had the procedure to try to unblock your tubes, two in vitro attempts, and I suspect the usual temperature taking and ovulation charts before all this began."

Carrie nodded.

"You must want a child very much."

"I…we do."